101 NIGHTS

101 NIGHTS

CHRISTOPH SPIELBERG

Translated by Christoph Spielberg with
Christina Henry de Tessan

amazoncrossing

Text copyright © 2003 Christoph Spielberg
Translation copyright © 2013 Christoph Spielberg

101 Nights was first published in 2003 by Piper Verlag as *Denn wer zuletzt stirbt*. Translated from German by Christoph Spielberg with Christina Henry de Tessan. First published in English by AmazonCrossing in 2013.

Published by AmazonCrossing
PO Box 400818
Las Vegas, NV 89140

ISBN-13: 9781477805305
ISBN-10: 1477805303
Library of Congress Control Number: 2013900605

The following printout of an intercepted message is marked "SECRET SPOKE," indicating a low level of confidentiality for NSA documents.

From: NSA Bad Aibling Station, Germany
To: NSA Headquarters, Fort Meade, Maryland

Report 22-49876-451
Source: ECHELON
Technique: MEMEX
Original language: Arabic

From: Ministry of Foreign Affairs, Baghdad, Republic of Iraq
To: Nasif Hamdai, chargé d'affaires, Embassy of Republic of Iraq, Berlin, Germany

Text: Shipment from Damascus. Airport TXL (Berlin/Germany), flight LH 1600 from Frankfurt. Arrival 17:05 local time. Report immediately: confirm arrival of shipment; recipient of shipment; final destination of shipment.

Analysis / evaluation NSA: pending

CHAPTER 1

By the time Celine finally returned from Baghdad, we had been separated for one hundred and one days. And one hundred and one nights. Not that we would have spent every one of those days together, or every one of those nights. We'd been a couple too long for that sort of thing. But one hundred and one days meant fourteen weekends that we hadn't kicked off with our regular Saturday breakfast together, and fourteen Sunday nights without the fun of cooking dinner side by side. My initial benevolence toward her project had quickly turned into anxious waiting, and finally, during the last two weeks, into an awful certainty. But with Celine finally returning to Berlin, I was strangely indifferent to her coming home. Of course, I went to the airport anyway.

Lufthansa flight 1600 from Frankfurt hit Runway 08 at 5:11 p.m., only six minutes late. A little tip to the right, instantly corrected by the autopilot, followed by a small cloud of rubber and dust as the landing gear touched the tarmac. As long as I'm not on board myself, I'm quite sure that flying is the safest and most convenient form of transport in the world. Celine always loved it.

At Gate 12, I had noticed a little old woman staring out at the runway. She was holding her purse tightly and standing beside her husband, a man with a militarylike bearing and an air of stoicism. I recognized Celine's parents right away. Hard to believe that they were just a little more than ten years older than I was.

I had given them a small nod, and then kept my distance. After all, it was their daughter coming back. They had arrived in Berlin two days earlier to wait for her. As the plane rolled toward the gate, an official-looking man approached them, said a few words, and led them out of my field of vision.

I hadn't dressed up to welcome Celine home. I knew that wouldn't bother her, nor would she care that I hadn't brought her flowers. She would, however, be annoyed by the Bundesgrenzschutz, our armed border police. These young men, barely beyond puberty, were all over the terminal. With their machine guns ready, they eyed me suspiciously, looking for the hand grenade or the surface-to-air missile I might be hiding under my winter coat. As a result of warnings from Washington and the latest al-Qaida video, security measures had been stepped up again. The tension was palpable.

The first passengers hastily disembarked—mostly business-men with their briefcases, and their parking tickets from the morning already in hand—and walked briskly toward the parking garage. I watched the luggage surfacing from the belly of the Airbus onto a conveyor belt. A lot of suitcases, of course, then a random surfboard and a pair of skis, followed by a few baby strollers.

After the conveyor belt was taken away, a forklift appeared, and its metal bars were raised to the luggage flap. Working carefully, the baggage handlers positioned a zinc coffin on the forks, and the driver slowly lowered it to the ground.

Celine's parents had reappeared, and were standing quietly beside the big airplane, a few feet behind the man who had just picked them up in the reception area. The forklift curved around slowly and disappeared with its load under the terminal, followed by the couple, who had suddenly aged so quickly. Their daughter had come home.

At Berlin's Tegel Airport, air freight from outside Germany was handled directly beneath the passenger terminal. They were probably opening Celine's coffin to make sure that it wasn't filled with poison gas or drugs from Iraq. Though the era of using coffins as a means of transporting such goodies was long past, customs agents perhaps counted on there being a few nostalgic types among Baghdad's drug lords.

I went to get my car and left Celine's parents to cope with their pain and suffering alone. They had made it clear that claiming the coffin was exclusively their business, and that my presence was uncalled for. They probably blamed me for Celine's trip to Baghdad—and, hence, for its fatal conclusion. Wrongly so, however, as the whole undertaking had been Celine's idea and hers alone. But it made no difference anymore.

I had hardly even known her parents. I had accompanied Celine to their row house in Hamburg-Bergedorf only once. It was at Christmas and had ended in a big fight between mother and daughter.

"If that's the case, then why doesn't that doctor marry you then?" I heard from downstairs as I wrapped my gift for Celine with totally ecologically unacceptable silver wrapping paper. "It's about time you got your life sorted out!"

This from the people who still prided themselves on the fact that years ago they had hidden a member of the Red Army Faction, Germany's leftist urban guerilla group, from the police!

"'That doctor' is going to marry me just as little as I am going to marry him."

At Celine's urging, we packed that very night and returned to Berlin. After that, I had encountered her parents only once more, at the funeral of some Kurt or Fritz, Celine's favorite uncle.

In the airport parking lot, I donated the five euros the machine asked for, gave a friendly wave to the surveillance camera, and got on the freeway. I wouldn't be going back to the clinic. Instead, I planned to drive straight home and put some Mozart on, anything so long as it was cheerful. Maybe the violin concertos or *Così fan tutte*. Grief is sad enough as it is.

CHAPTER 2

But there was to be no Mozart that night. No sooner had I fished out the remote control for the CD player from my ever-growing collection of remote controls—only after the radio started blasting and the TV sprang to life against my wishes—than the doorbell rang.

Two neatly dressed men were at the door. They asked if they could speak to me for a minute. I explained that I didn't need a magazine subscription, more insurance, or a new religion. And that it was a bad night to ask for a donation, no matter what it was for.

"We don't want to sell you anything. And we didn't come to ask for a donation. We have a few questions concerning Ms. Celine Bergkamp, if you don't mind."

They both waved plastic ID cards meaningfully under my nose. That was a mistake, because right before they did that, I had realized that I felt rather lonely and would have welcomed some company, even if that had meant subscribing to some magazine. But thanks to the ID cards, I was on my guard.

"Who can I call to verify your credentials?"

"Just dial 226 570 and ask for the officer on duty. He will confirm our identities."

Normally I'm rather gullible. So perhaps my reaction was due to Celine and the coffin.

"I'd rather you told me who sent you. I'll look up the telephone number myself."

After some page turning, I found the entry for "Bundesamt für Verfassungsschutz," the German equivalent of the National Security Branch of the FBI. The phone book showed the address of the Berlin office and, yes, 226 570 was indeed the correct phone number. For some reason I found it comforting to live in a country whose intelligence service was listed in the phone book. Did they also have a website with photos of all their employees? Or at least an image of the "employee of the month"—whoever had nailed the most terrorists lately? In any event, when I dialed 226 570, I was assured that the gentlemen in my home, Jablonske and Waldeck, had indeed come to see me on official business and that the Federal Republic of Germany would appreciate my cooperation.

The Federal Republic of Germany for her part hadn't shown a great deal of cooperation when I was anxiously looking into Celine's disappearance in Iraq. But I was interested in what these gentlemen wanted to know. And what they might tell me.

They were still standing in front of my door, looking at a sticker showing two fat-nosed cops that said, "Sorry, we have to stay outside." Celine had put it there long ago, and after my experience with Chief Inspector Czarnowske the year before, I had made a point of leaving it there.

When I finally asked them in, Jablonske and Waldeck looked around with more than mere professional curiosity. I knew the look. A plumber who had checked a dripping radiator last month had put it like this: "Interesting to see how a doctor lives." He was probably just as disappointed then as the gentlemen from the Verfassungsschutz seemed now. What did people expect? An after-hours operating room in the kitchen? An illegal drug laboratory? Gold-plated faucets?

Jablonske helped himself to the next-to-last Kleenex on my desk and blew his nose at length, apologetically murmuring, "Damn sinuses." Perhaps he was hoping for some free medical advice. In vain. His colleague, Waldeck, started right in on the interrogation.

"What exactly is the nature of your relationship to Ms. Bergkamp?"

This struck me as a reasonable question. I understood that the two gentlemen had to weigh carefully just how much of their knowledge they would share with me. Then again, how much did they already know of my relationship to Celine? Or, for that matter, how did they know about our relationship at all? When I asked them, their answer was evasive. But of course they knew about Celine and me. After all, I had been a near-constant guest at the Ministry of Foreign Affairs ever since my last contact with Celine, when she'd called me from the Turkish border before crossing into the Kurdish part of Iraq. The same undersecretary there had assured me on countless occasions that the Federal Republic was doing everything possible, but...

"Celine Bergkamp and I were friends."

"Just friends?"

"Very good friends. Close friends. We have known each other for years."

"But you didn't live together?"

"No. But surely you know that Celine lives just across the street...I mean, lived."

"Close friends...for years...I understand..."

Apparently not, judging by his next question.

"And why weren't you married?"

The question remained unanswered. Had these two in fact been sent by Celine's parents? I had to smile at the thought. I was pretty sure that when the Verfassungsschutz fed Celine's name into their computer system, a little red light had started blinking: Years ago, Celine's parents had thought of themselves as revolutionaries, spearheads of a new social order. The climax of their revolutionary activities had been when they hid that member of the Red Army Faction from the police for a night or two. If that was what had prompted the Verfassungsschutz to pay me a visit, I found that really quite funny. Like so many others, Celine's parents' grand plans to reform the system from within had gradually been whittled down and, perhaps without even realizing it, they had become part of that very system's middle-class bourgeoisie.

The next question made it clear that, yes, there had indeed been a red light next to her name.

"So, Dr. Hoffmann, do you agree with Ms. Bergkamp's political views?"

Celine's political views had been subject to change daily, and were at least as confused and contradictory as my ideas about the first ten milliseconds after the Big Bang, or the question of how a zipper actually works.

"Do *you* know Ms. Bergkamp's political views?"

Jablonske was still busy with his summer flu, so Waldeck carried on.

"According to our information, Ms. Bergkamp was rather active in several political groups."

I suppressed my growing anger.

"Celine Bergkamp always took a stand for justice and human rights, and equal opportunities for all. Those rights are an integral part of our constitution, aren't they?" I thought that was a nice response to throw at the pair, since the literal translation of *Bundesamt für Verfassungsschutz* is "office for the Defense of the Constitution." I continued with this line of reasoning. "She was quite active in Pro Asyl, an organization that fights for the rights of political refugees, as you certainly know. Do you consider that an unconstitutional activity? Does someone who fights for the rights of asylum seekers act against the 'free democratic order' of the Federal Republic of Germany?"

"Well, there are photos of Ms. Bergkamp at various antiglobalization demonstrations. A number of those resulted in considerable violence against the police."

"Yes, Celine always sided with the weak and disenfranchised. To her, globalization was simply the continuation of Western colonialism at a broader level. Does that make her a bomber in Baghdad?"

Waldeck remained undeterred.

"And you yourself, Dr. Hoffmann? Are you in sympathy with throwing stones and Molotov cocktails at the police?"

It was rapidly becoming clear what this was all about: If I was "in sympathy," I was close to what the Verfassungsschutz called a "sympathizer," only an inch away from being a terrorist myself. These two had not come to share with me whatever they knew about what had happened to Celine in Iraq. They were there to smoke out a terror cell! I got up.

"Excuse my naiveté, gentlemen. For a moment I actually assumed that you could tell me something about how and why Ms. Bergkamp had to die. If that is not the case, I am sure that you have more important matters to attend to tonight. So please don't let me stop you."

Waldeck jumped up, his face bright red, ready to say—or rather, shout—something at me. He was probably about to point out that there was more than one way they could get people like me to talk, that they could take me to their office, even lock me up for a night. But Jablonske gave him a quick look that stopped Waldeck before he'd even begun. Jablonske snorted again loudly and at length, inspected the result in my last Kleenex, and cleared his throat.

"Dr. Hoffmann, in our work, as in any other, we can become professionally blind at times. As a result, our questions are sometimes misunderstood."

Jablonske was clearly criticizing his colleague, making it easy for me to side with him. Perhaps I wouldn't charge him for the Kleenex. He went on.

"Why don't we just start at the beginning again. We are, of course, just as eager as you are to discover what happened to Ms. Bergkamp, believe me. That's why we need some background information from you. For instance, how did she organize her transport of relief supplies in the first place, why Kurdish Iraq, who helped her, et cetera. Would you be willing to give us some of that information?"

I'm not dumb. These two were playing good cop/bad cop, of course, but I decided to play along. Perhaps they would eventually reveal something worth knowing. I sat back down. So did Waldeck.

"I already explained to you that Celine always went to great lengths for the underprivileged. In the last year she has worked very actively for asylum seekers from Kurdistan, which is how she learned so much about their situation inside Iraq. Among other things, she learned how little the Kurds had profited from the UN Oil-for-Food Program. Most of that money went directly to Saddam Hussein, into gold and marble for his palaces, and to his friends. The thirteen percent that Saddam was required to hand off to the Kurds was nowhere near enough. They'd have starved if they hadn't smuggled their oil to Turkey. That's why Celine began to collect medical samples, first from my hospital, then from other hospitals and private practitioners. That's how it all started. It then expanded to include used medical instruments and equipment. She even managed to take our complete X-ray apparatus with her. And, of course, we also raised money."

I saw no reason to mention that she had also saved the hospital some big money, which otherwise would have gone toward disposing of the old X-ray equipment properly.

"That was certainly nice of her. But she could have handed all that over to some experienced organization, like the Red Cross. Those people handle transports like that all the time."

"Celine was strictly against acting through those 'experienced organizations.' Even if everything goes according to plan, too much money is lost in administration. And many people make a fortune from things like expired canned food and decommissioned army tents. Then the rest of the aid somehow disappears on-site."

"But still, to organize a transport across most of Europe and then to lead the way herself..."

"Believe me, I too disliked that part of her plan. But again, Celine held very definite views. She'd learned that the 'experienced organizations' often commission these transports to people who normally make their living on less humanitarian assignments such as drug shipments, people trafficking, and illegal arms transports. It comes down to this: you just don't know Celine Bergkamp! When she signed up for a training program to get her commercial driver's license, it was clear that nothing would stop her from going herself."

"But you see pictures of Red Cross convoys in those areas all the time."

"What you see are pictures of trucks with a Red Cross painted on their tarp. I'm talking about the drivers. Of course you can also find official representatives of these organizations on-site. But you'll have to look for them in the lobby or at the bar of your nearest five-star air-conditioned hotel, off-limits for locals."

I knew that I was being a bit unfair, that there were plenty of people from relief agencies and NGOs sweating their asses off in refugee camps. But what I had said was true of most of the higher-ups. I had seen those people myself when I'd attended a medical convention on AIDS in Nairobi the year before. Of course, we doctors hadn't actually stayed in a backyard shack ourselves.

"And how did Ms. Bergkamp get hold of the trucks for her convoy?"

Again I had to smile to myself when I remembered the vehicles Celine and Heiner had originally considered for their project: decommissioned light trucks from UPS and the like, which friends of theirs had converted into campers and roach coaches.

"How far do you think you'll get with these rust buckets?" I had asked them.

"Have you got something better?"

"Let me think…"

I thought of Mr. Sommer.

"At the time," I told the two defenders of our constitution, "the hospital needed to place an order for the installation of new gas supplies for our surgery department. New pumps and pipes for oxygen, compressed air, narcotic gases, and so on. Sommer Inc. specializes in this sort of thing. Of course, we never said explicitly that he would only get the contract if he helped Celine, but Mr. Sommer got the message. In any case, he got the contract, and Celine got two of their big company trucks full of diesel and free of charge. Plus a complete water purification plant, only half of which she managed to take along this time. She planned to take the other half on her next trip."

I grinned as I recalled how we had talked Sommer into the deal. My smile probably looked suspicious to Waldeck, as he decided it was time for the bad cop to join the interrogation again. "A real philanthropist, your Mr. Sommer, huh?"

"I don't know if he's a philanthropist. But he's certainly a clever businessman. He knew that, in addition to the new gas installations for surgery, the hospital would soon be needing new gas lines, and pumps for the wards, too. Which is a pretty big project."

"OK. So we have two trucks now and your friend with a brand-new commercial driver's license. Who drove the other truck?"

Yes, that was another thing I didn't like about Celine making the drive herself.

"A friend of Ms. Bergkamp's from her charity, Pro Asyl."

This friend was Heiner, a good-looking man somewhat younger than myself, who Celine had increasingly mentioned as an authority whenever we didn't agree on something. Heiner had also vanished in Iraq, but so far his body hadn't turned up. It seemed to me that Waldeck's lower lip flinched when I mentioned Pro Asyl again. Perhaps it was that name that prompted him to go into his bad-cop routine again.

"Dr. Hoffmann, what a heartwarming story you are serving up here! Selfless helpers who leave everything behind—their jobs, their friends, their family—to drive two trucks across Europe with a few items others could have transported far more efficiently. Did you really think we would buy this fairy tale?"

For a moment I looked at the world through the eyes of Herr Waldeck: I saw a world in which nobody spends his annual vacation washing the sick in the slums of Calcutta or vaccinating kids on the streets of Lima, where no engineers would volunteer to dig water wells in Africa for nothing more than a thank-you. It was a sad world indeed. Had Waldeck been born with this outlook? Was this attitude a basic requirement for officers in Germany's Verfassungsschutz? Or did they acquire it gradually on the job, as a sort of vocational disease? Whatever the situation, he had never met Celine and her occasionally naive but always sincere willingness to help.

I had a closer look at his colleague. In him I detected an air of serenity, with a tint of regret, like a good uncle, who would read a good-night story to his niece or nephew. Did that serenity mean that he had seen and heard it all—all the misery and lies out there— and that nothing could shock him anymore? Would he, on orders, kill me with the same expression of deep regret? But I realized I likely had far too dramatic a notion of how his department worked. These men probably only ran around killing people in the movies. In reality they likely spent the bulk of their time searching for lost files, or creating new files by clumsily typing reports into their computers with two fingers—or trying to work the bill from their last family outing into their expense account. That is, if they weren't hard at work interrogating a prime suspect like me.

Waldeck repeated his question: Did I really think he was naive enough to believe my story?

"What is it exactly that bothers you so much about my narrative?"

"Dr. Hoffmann, OK, let's assume that you and your friend Ms. Bergkamp had only the most noble motives. In the beginning at least. Maybe that was so. But don't forget, we at the Verfassungsschutz know a bit about Eastern Europe and the Middle East. What you're trying to tell me is that your Ms. Bergkamp can go meandering through all these respectable countries, among them Serbia and Bulgaria, with two truckloads full of valuable medications and medical equipment without the consent of anybody on the inside there? Without any connections to influential people in these countries? And beyond that, that she would finally arrive in Kurdish Iraq with her cargo undisturbed? Now really!"

Waldeck was not all wrong. The cargo had not, in fact, been quite complete upon Celine's arrival in Kurdistan. And his suspicions about the transports through the Balkans were correct. But again, he didn't know Celine. The e-mail she'd sent me from the Bulgarian border summed up her approach best: They would only let her pass, they said, if they got half her load. But after a night of poker and five bottles of slivovitz, the barriers were lifted, and the transported goods were permitted to pass through untouched. Again, you had to know Celine to believe this story. They wouldn't have opened the border for me after five *crates* of slivovitz. Nor, for that matter, would they have done so for my two friends from the Verfassungsschutz. But details like that were none of their business. I simply referred to "Ms. Bergkamp's extraordinary persuasiveness."

Waldeck wasn't satisfied with that, however. Not at all. He simply became all the more convinced of his own theory.

"Let me tell you how you get through with a transport like that down there. Actually you mentioned it yourself: drugs! There's always enough space for a kilo or two on a truck. All in the name of a good cause, naturally."

Since when had the Verfassungsschutz been interested in drugs? As far as I knew, this had become the new sport of the Bundesnachrichtendienst, or BND—Germany's CIA equivalent—since they'd run out of Communist spies to catch. But perhaps not being in the drug business was precisely the reason for Waldeck's absurd insinuation.

"Oh—I must have missed some new development. So nowadays drugs are smuggled *from* Germany *into* Iraq?"

Jablonske came to his colleague's rescue.

"We're talking about the other way around of course."

Waldeck gladly accepted the assist. "We think that the relief mission was just a pretense for bringing drugs into the country on the way back. As they say: no point in an empty run! Or, to look at it more benevolently, a way to finance the next aid convoy."

"Now I get it! So once in Iraq, Celine got into a big fight about the drugs, and she got so mad that she exploded a bomb, killing herself in the process. That's all very logical, crystal clear, in fact. How else could it have happened?"

By that point, Jablonske had used up all my Kleenex and his sniffling was growing increasingly irritating. I got him a roll of paper towels from the kitchen and grabbed a beer for myself. That gave the two of them enough time to come up with a new theory.

"Drugs aren't the only contraband transported across the Balkans. A few kilos of Semtex from the Czech Republic are also always welcome."

To be fair, we operated the same way in the medical field: if we find our first hypothesis wrong, we rearrange the patient's symptoms and laboratory results to see if a new diagnosis will fit. I was sure then that my visitors were just groping in the dark. Still, with their latest theory they had come the tiniest bit closer to the truth. Nobody had tried to slip Celine a few kilos of that convenient Czech explosive Semtex. But about two hundred miles after Ankara, she and Heiner had been asked to please bring "humanitarian help for our Kurdish friends from Ansar al-Islam" in the form of four wooden boxes neatly painted with the Red Crescent logo and full to the brim of hand grenades. Those boxes were now safely on the bottom of the Euphrates.

"Anything else you can think of?" I asked Waldeck. "How about some nice biological weapons for Saddam Hussein from our hospital laboratory? Plague or anthrax, for example? Or poison gas?"

Jablonske once again tried to take the benevolent old uncle approach while quietly studying my bookshelves. What did he expect to find there? Edifying literature like *Handcrafting Bombs for Dummies* or *The Beginner Terrorist's Manual*?

"Dear Dr. Hoffmann, we are sure that your friend's first priority was humanitarian. We are very sorry about whatever happened after that. We just want to find out what it was."

Now Waldeck tried to assist.

"Perhaps this is a good time to remind you that we have a leniency program under the latest antiterrorism act. Not complete immunity from prosecution, to be sure—we're not in America after all—but charges can be significantly reduced, as can possible sentences."

They both beamed at me as though they were boys looking into Santa's bag—bad boys who actually didn't deserve it.

"What my colleague means," Jablonske specified, "is that 'murder' can turn into 'physical injury resulting from negligence' or 'aggravated robbery' suddenly can be reduced to 'simple shoplifting.'"

"Fine. But I didn't murder anybody. I haven't even stolen anything lately."

I thought it prudent to exhibit ignorance. Paragraph 211, first-degree murder, paragraph 212, second-degree murder, paragraph 224, aggravated battery: my guests probably had no idea that, as a doctor these days, you needed intimate knowledge of the criminal code to spend at least part of your life outside of jail.

"I was just giving examples," Jablonske said indignantly, looking annoyed. "Do you know, by chance, what you get for supporting a terrorist group?"

I realized we would never become friends. I made the pair watch me as I grabbed myself another beer. Their yearning looks when I had gotten my first one hadn't been lost on me. I popped the bottle cap and took a long quaff.

Waldeck gave his colleague a quick nod, and Jablonske tossed a business card at me.

"If something helpful occurs to you, you can reach us at that number anytime."

Being a doctor means helping regardless of how you feel about the person, so in return for his business card, I offered Jablonske my paper towels. Which he accepted. He was almost out of the door when he turned to me, Columbo-style, with a final question. A very strange question.

"Have you had any contact with your friend Ms. Bergkamp since the bombing in Baghdad?"

I could only shake my head. The pair finally left. I was sure that they would be stopping for a beer at the first opportunity.

CHAPTER 3

Was I sufficiently mourning Celine's death? I think so, but how can you ever be sure of the right words for your feelings? You'll never know what somebody else is really feeling when they speak of mourning, of love, of grief. What I felt was a shattering loss, a void, a sense that a part of me had been amputated. Only when I saw Celine's coffin on that forklift had I finally been forced to accept the reality of her death. Up until then, I had still thought it must be a terrible misunderstanding, a case of mistaken identity or some hideous Iraqi propaganda coup. Then I finally began to grasp that Celine would never again laugh at my tasteless jokes, that we would never again cook together, never again break into somebody's office or rifle through filthy garbage looking for evidence, as we had in the past. Perhaps the pain from the amputation would recede with time, but at the moment that seemed an unrealistic hope.

How was I to fill this emptiness? To follow the well-meant suggestion to "take a few days off" would only make me feel worse, that I was sure of. Never before had I so looked forward to going to work. There, the patients simply expected their doctor to function and not to be distracted by his own problems. So the next morning, as I was getting ready to once again take up the ongoing struggle against disease, death, and the absurdities of our health-care system, I was thankful for the fact that I still had at least one frontline to fight on with some chance of success from time to time.

That wasn't a given. Last year, South Berlin Hospital's future seemed doomed, and its shutdown looked inevitable. The city government had to somehow compensate for the losses the mainly government-owned Bank of Berlin had incurred as a result of a slew of shady property investments. And of course it would have been inappropriate to ask the managers responsible for these transactions or the profiteers from these deals to help with the recovery of the €20 billion-plus that had been lost. To close down yet another city hospital seemed a far better alternative. "No problem," chorused the other Berlin hospitals in unison, differentiated only by the volume of their responses. They could hardly wait to take over our patients and whatever else would be left from a liquidated South Berlin Hospital.

Our clinic was ultimately saved by the newly created Vitalis Clinics Ltd., which bought South Berlin Hospital and all the other community-run hospitals from the Berlin government for one euro. Sure, that wouldn't restore the billions lost by their bank, but it would save the city millions in personnel expenses and maintenance costs alone—at least, that was how the government defended the deal. Of course, the net property value alone made this an excellent bargain for Vitalis, which was fine with me and my colleagues, as long as the buyout saved our jobs.

So after all the turbulence, South Berlin Hospital was on its way back to being a normal hospital with a proven pecking order. We had department heads again, as well as residents and interns, and everybody finally knew who could kick whom in the ass. However, the internal medicine department, which I'd had the honor of working in for the last ten years, was still looking for a new department head. Professor Kleinweg had filled that position on a provisional basis. His real job was as the department head of another hospital in the Vitalis group; our contact with him was limited to a guest appearance every Thursday morning, so that our patients wouldn't miss their weekly show, "Rounds by the Chief." Responsibility for the daily routine fell to the most senior resident: Yours truly. Dr. Hoffmann. Me.

As usual, I was confronted upon arrival with enough questions to answer and decisions to make to keep me sufficiently busy for the better part of the morning. Should we try yet another round of antibiotics on Herr Krauskopf, or should the surgeons finally tackle his infected kidney? Did Herr Schlups need a pacemaker? With Mrs. Zachels, the critical question was whether she belonged as our patient in internal medicine because of her heart condition, or whether she should be primarily the responsibility of the gynecologists due to her bleeding uterine myoma. Of course I decided in our best interest, which, I was sure, was in the best interest of Mrs. Zachels as well. The winning argument was simple and comprehensible even to the gynecologists: it was easier to march three stories down daily (from gynecology to internal medicine) than three stories up (from internal medicine to gynecology). When the gynecologists—after some serious thinking—found the flaw in my rational argumentation, I told them that they could see her on their way to lunch, when they would have to come down to our floor anyway.

Between making decisions, postponing them, and revising prior wrong decisions, it was noon before I ran into Beate, who had been our hospital's CEO for some years.

"Hello, Felix."

She greeted me with a big hug.

It was hard to say which of us had been closer to Celine. Both of us had known her for years. But perhaps the question was moot. I assumed that there had been a Beate-Celine and a

Felix-Celine. Both versions must have had a lot in common, but I figured she revealed different sides of herself to each of us.

Beate and I had planned to go to the airport together, but Vitalis had scheduled a meeting of all its hospitals' CEOs on short notice. No chance of Beate skipping that one—her colleagues would have agreed in no time which Vitalis hospital could manage with a lower budget and perhaps even without its own CEO.

"How was the airport?"

"Her parents took care of everything. This has put years on them."

"I'm not surprised. What can be more terrible than burying your own child? Anything we can do for these people?"

"I don't know. They never liked me much before. Now they're cutting themselves off from me altogether. Perhaps you could talk to them. We need to know their plans for the burial, what to do with Celine's stuff, things like that."

Our conversation was typical of the sort Beate and I had when talking about Celine lately. We kept to technicalities, or changed the subject, both unsure how much the other could handle—not to mention what we could take ourselves. Beate scribbled a few words in her notebook. She was, unlike Celine, very organized.

"How did that CEO conference go?"

"You would never guess, Felix. Costs per patient too high, costs per doctor too high. More cost control, please!"

I had no trouble picturing it. Herr Hirth, CEO of all Vitalis hospitals, was a statistics fan and loved PowerPoint presentations. Naturally, he was always eager to find new ways to cut corners.

"But there's an easy solution for that, Beate. The hospital should just hire more doctors. Then costs per doctor will automatically decline. And the beauty of it is you save a lot of overtime pay."

Beate gave me a weak smile while scribbling another note in her organizer. Surely not to remind herself to hire more doctors.

"At the moment Vitalis is preoccupied with their rehabilitation clinics, so we're not in the line of fire for now. But something new came up. Actually, the bureaucrats down at City Hall came up with it: they're calling it 'emergency management.'" Beate pointed at the ring binder she was carrying. "Are our emergency plans up to date? Has terrorism been taken into account? Could patients be taken hostage? Could dangerous or infectious material be stolen from our laboratories?"

I knew we had a pretty good emergency plan. It had even been put to the test once when the Libyans exploded a bomb in the La Belle disco, killing three and wounding over two hundred, many of them American soldiers. It had worked well then, but that had been more than a decade ago. I knew that the plans had not been updated since. The plan described how to manage a sudden and massive influx of patients, but it didn't account for the possibility that the hospital itself could come under attack. These days anybody could enter or leave the hospital any time of day; it was less secure than your average midrange hotel. Only a few weeks before, I'd told an outpatient, "Whatever your problem is, it's certainly not somatic," and the next day he threw a stink bomb into my ward. I knew a time would come when people like him would upgrade their armory. I figured you probably couldn't craft a nuclear bomb from what you found in our department of nuclear medicine, but I anticipated serious trouble should some radical animal rights activist set free the bacteria and viruses from the incubators in the microbiology lab.

By that time, we'd reached Beate's office, and she invited me in. I was pretty sure that she wasn't just making conversation when she mentioned the city government's new interest in our emergency plan. I was already considering which of my younger colleagues I could pass the project to when Beate fished a second folder from her desk, making the pile of papers around it collapse.

As I helped her restore some kind of order to the towering stacks, Beate continued.

"Our dear government's concerns go beyond updating contingency plans. After 9/11, they think we have to be prepared for anything. Do we have enough banked blood? Enough infusions even if part of the storage system is destroyed or contaminated? How many days do our emergency generators have fuel for? This folder is full of questions like that."

Just as I had feared, she shoved the folder in my direction.

"Could you have a look at it? It's full of medical terminology I know nothing about." She paused. "But of course, if at the moment you..."

"No, it's OK. Actually I'm thankful for any kind of distraction."

Plus I could still let some ambitious young colleague do the work.

"Thank you," Beate said. "The mayor's office has even appointed a coordinator we're supposed to work with. He was at the conference. Someone from the city's health department, a certain Dr. Zentis."

"Dr. Zentis?"

"Yes, I think that was his name. It must be in those papers somewhere. Quite a windbag, if you ask me. Had to give his two cents on everything, spitting out numbers and statistics I think he just made up on the spot. But everybody was hanging on his every word as though he were proclaiming the gospel. You know the type, don't you?"

Beate was right. However, I didn't only know the type, I knew the prototype itself, the personified model of all windbags and machinators: I had the honor of knowing Dr. Zentis personally. Beate wasn't aware of that, having started at South Berlin Hospital only after Zentis had been kicked out. Our then department head, Professor Kindel, had sweetened the deal for Zentis a little by certifying that he'd completed his training in internal medicine. That wasn't actually the case, but he'd been willing to do anything to get rid of the man. In return, the fellow had pressed charges, alleging several cases of mistreatment during his time at South Berlin Hospital, and later even charged that his colleagues had been after his dear life. His claims weren't entirely unfounded. He just forgot to report the right cases, the ones that had prompted him to get the ax. Beate's term *windbag* was accurate, but far understated.

"Well, have fun then," Beate said.

I stood up and tucked the files under my arm. When would Beate and I be able to really talk about Celine again? When would I not welcome extra work anymore, just to keep my mind from wandering? It was only Tuesday, but already I was afraid of the free weekend coming up.

"Beate, do you want to come have dinner at my place on Sunday? Only one condition: don't meddle with my cooking."

Beate was well aware of the Celine-Felix weekend ritual: breakfast together on Saturdays, dinner together on Sundays.

"My cooking isn't as bad as Celine's!"

True, that was hardly possible.

"OK, then. You bring the wine."

On the way back to my ward, I stopped to tell the surgeons that they wouldn't be getting Krauskopf's kidney anytime soon.

"There's a new aminoglycoside on the market, and we want to give it a chance."

To my surprise, there was no protest from the surgeons; indeed, just the opposite.

"Fine with us. We need to delay all the operations we can at the moment anyway. Just take a look around—this was supposed to have been done weeks ago!"

Walls that had just been finished had been pried open again, and the pipes that had just been installed were in the process of being torn out.

"Those guys from Sommer Inc. managed to hook up the laughing gas to the compressed air pipes. And if you need distilled water, no problem—but you get it boiling hot! For the moment, we're doing all urgent procedures in the gynecologists' OR—so keep your antibiotics warm."

The surgeons were not referring to my Herr Krauskopf and his infected kidney. They meant that sharing the OR with, of all people, their colleagues from gynecology—known for its higher germ load—would put their patients at risk for all kinds of infections.

"None of this is our fault. The construction plans of the building we got from you were totally outdated." The voice came from behind me. I turned to see who it was.

Herr Sobotka had joined us—without having been asked. He was the on-site construction manager and loyal agent of Sommer's interests. His company had gotten the contract for the reinstallation of the pumps and pipes not only because they were one of the most prominent manufacturers of all things related to medical or technical gases, but also because they'd agreed to have their own people perform all the necessary installations.

Of course, the two trucks and the water purification plant for Celine's project had also played a role in Beate's decision to go with Sommer Inc. Had I known Herr Sobotka at the time, however, I think I would have vetoed Sommer Inc. and helped Celine to look for assistance elsewhere.

Sobotka was well aware of his imposing stature and its intimidating effect. He didn't have to spell anything out to get the point across that we shouldn't even think of asking for discounted terms on the grounds that he and his people hadn't met their deadline.

Herr Sobotka was somebody I never wanted to meet in a dark alley.

Since I had strongly supported Sommer's bid for the contract (for obvious reasons), I felt at least partly responsible for the mess the surgeons were faced with. Back in my office, I called Sommer Inc., and after some explanations and being put on hold, the big boss himself got on the phone.

"I don't know if the delay has anything to do with outdated plans, but I will look into the matter myself, Dr. Hoffmann, and see what can be done. More importantly, I am terribly sorry about what happened to your friend, Ms. Bergkamp. If only I hadn't given her those damn trucks!"

"Herr Sommer, you met Celine. You must know that she would have gotten to Kurdistan one way or another—if not in your trucks, then in other trucks, or by mule if she'd had to. None of this is your fault."

It was kind of Herr Sommer to express his sympathy, but I had some difficulty believing that the businessman would suffer from too much guilt. What he probably meant was that he hoped that this wouldn't hurt his present and future dealings with Vitalis Clinics Ltd. After all, the water purification plant project was scheduled to get under way soon.

My thoughts wandered for a moment, as they often did lately. I had just started listening again when Sommer said, "And of course, if there is anything else I can do for you…"

As a matter of fact, there was.

"Now that you mention it, Herr Sommer, I was wondering whether, with your excellent network, you might be able to get someone of some importance at the Iraqi embassy to meet with me?"

Of everything I had told—or rather, *not* told—my two guests from our inland security service, this had been true: never in a million years would Celine run around with a bomb, either in

Baghdad or anywhere else. I knew that finding out what really happened would help me cope with my loss.

"I'll have to call you back about that, Dr. Hoffmann. Let me see what I can do."

I was sure that Herr Sommer would come through for me, as it was he and his contacts who had gotten us most of the necessary papers and documentation for Celine and Heiner's journey across Eastern Europe and even into Iraq.

Memo

From:	Foreign Office, Federal Republic of Germany, StS von Schmöllendorf
To:	Embassy of the Federal Republic of Germany, Amman, Hashemite Kingdom of Jordan, department Iraq, ad interim Herr LR Drebner.
Ref:	Your next consultation at Iraqi Ministry of Foreign Affairs

Ref. 1 (planned visit of a delegation of high-level businessmen from Germany to Iraq): Please stress that, due to the current political situation and in order to not irritate the US, the visit has been postponed, but not canceled. The Federal Republic of Germany remains greatly interested not only in continuing, but strengthening business ties with the Republic of Iraq. This should be made clear not only to government officials but in particular to local managers and technocrats who will remain in office even after a possible change of regime. Out of deference to the US, German government–guaranteed Hermes export credits are temporarily on hold. Alternate procedures are being worked out discreetly with Deutsche Bank.

Ref. 2 (German national Celine Ulrike Bergkamp): Assure Iraqi authorities that Ms. Bergkamp's activities in Iraq were of an exclusively personal nature. It is in the best interest of both the Federal Republic of Germany and the Republic of Iraq that this case should in no way disrupt the relations between the two countries.

Ref. 3 (Kurdish Iraq): The Federal Republic of Germany views the Republic of Iraq's relationship with her Kurdish citizens as a domestic issue concerning only Iraq. Our policy has always been one of noninterference in the internal affairs of other countries.

Germany's granting asylum to Kurdish people from Iraq is a consequence of solely humanitarian, not political, motives. Please make it clear once again to Iraqi authorities that Germany has a free press and that the German government has no influence over that press.

Ref. 4 (Iraq-US relations): The Federal Republic of Germany's position with regard to possible US military actions against Iraq is well known and remains unchanged.

CHAPTER 4

The Iraqi embassy was only a few blocks from where I lived. The stately but somewhat run-down mansion, built in the Wilhelminian style with a few touches of art nouveau, was situated on a street corner, which made it easier to keep it under surveillance.

Because it had been stormed and occupied for five or six hours some weeks earlier by a previously unknown group that called itself the Democratic Iraqi Opposition, a lonely policeman patrolled the street in front of it. Although I couldn't see the cameras, I was sure that our security people were monitoring the place on closed-circuit television. The quaint old days when inconspicuous ice-cream salesmen sold their product across the street irrespective of drenching rain or bone-chilling cold were long gone. The Iraqis had their own camera pointed at the entrance, one that was clearly visible. The German and Iraqi governments could have agreed to share a single camera, but that would kill jobs, which neither party cared to do—least of all the German security services, who still fought fiercely against any proposed post–Cold War staff reductions.

The night before, I had killed some time by browsing the folder that Beate had passed on to me. Entitled "Current state of and deficits in emergency management and antiterrorist protection in Berlin," it was packed with statistics, tables, and diagrams. My one-time colleague Dr. Zentis was in his element. According to him, abandoning the atomic bomb shelters and emergency hospitals beneath subway stations and shopping centers after the downfall of the Soviet Union had been overly hasty, as had been terminating the city's supply of emergency medications and food, which had been put in place after the Berlin blockade.

Zentis had not only mercilessly listed all of the existing plan's weak points, but, better still, he had all the solutions. I was surprised to note one thing, though: Zentis normally loved to cite himself. But in this paper he modestly withheld the part he had played in downsizing our city's medical contingency plan when he worked for the Berlin health department. The first meeting of the committee he had just created to secure our survival in case of catastrophe was two days away. I was already looking forward to it.

I arrived at the Iraqi embassy with a somewhat uneasy feeling—for this was, after all, the embassy of a rogue state, as the Americans called it. The thought of the German surveillance cameras reassured me. They would keep track of the people entering the building, wouldn't they?

In the lobby I passed through a metal detector, and then I was patted down. After that, it was all very straightforward.

Herr Sommer had kept his word, and I was received by the chargé d'affaires himself. Armani suit, crocodile-skin shoes, silk necktie. The effects of the UN embargo on Iraq were evidently of limited consequence to him. His boss, Saddam Hussein, smiled benevolently down on us from a large portrait on the wall.

The acting ambassador began by pointing out Germany's "positive role" in his country's "current problems" with the United States of America. I refrained from reminding him that much of that "positive role"—a euphemism for the fact that Germany had

agreed not to take part in a possible military action against Iraq—
was due to our upcoming elections and that I, like probably 99.9
percent of all Germans, still wished to see his criminal superass-
hole boss burn in hell. Instead, I brought our thus far one-sided
conversation around to Celine.

Yes, the acting ambassador said, he had read the report, and
he deeply regretted her fate, of course. But her death shouldn't
be blamed on his country, which had welcomed Ms. Bergkamp
as a guest and offered her every possible assistance with her
task.

Actually this was true. Celine and Heiner had somehow
managed to get permission to enter Kurdish Iraq through their
Kurdish friends here. But their official entry permit to Iraq had
been issued by the Ministry for Cultural Affairs and Information
in Baghdad, thanks to Herr Sommer's contacts. Although Kurdish
Iraq became autonomous after the Gulf War in 1991, Sommer
had insisted that they take the Iraqi paperwork with them, just
in case. "You know, anything can happen once you're under way,
right? In the end, Saddam's people are in control once you get
there," Sommer had warned Celine and Heiner.

"I certainly hope not," Celine had replied.

But I remembered how she had mentioned repeatedly that
not only the Kurds, but almost all of the Iraqis were held hostage by their freaked-out leader. Had she perhaps made use of her
Iraqi documents to expand the area of her mission? Had she in
fact gone on to Baghdad?

I asked the ambassador, "Are you sure that Ms. Bergkamp was
in Iraq proper? From what I understand, her mission was north
of the thirty-sixth parallel."

The acting ambassador gave me a wry smile. "The region
north of the thirty-sixth parallel is an integral part of the Republic
of Iraq, Dr. Hoffmann. It is partly in the hands of rebels and terrorists, which is most regrettable. Unfortunately, Germany isn't

willing to help us with this problem and even grants asylum to these terrorists."

"Is this—the position of my government regarding the Kurds in Iraq—the reason Ms. Bergkamp had to die?"

I tried to shake the ambassador out of his complacency, but he kept his diplomatic countenance.

"Dr. Hoffmann, I think you are well aware of the circumstances under which Ms. Bergkamp lost her life. She not only gravely violated our laws, she committed an act of terrorism. She abused her right to hospitality and betrayed the goodwill we had welcomed her with."

"That is precisely what I refuse to believe. She would never do anything like that. I have known Ms. Bergkamp for years."

Even if Celine had gone on the Baghdad for some reason, would she have dropped a bomb there? Nonsense!

"I am afraid," the ambassador continued, "that Ms. Bergkamp not only transported humanitarian goods to these terrorists. Unfortunately, she also cooperated with them. She made that clear herself."

Complete bullshit. But wait a second.

"She made that clear herself? When was she supposed to have done that? I was told that Ms. Bergkamp died instantaneously, torn apart by a bomb?"

The ambassador gave me an annoyed look.

"You misunderstand me, Doctor. She made it clear by her actions in Baghdad. You must agree that she could hardly have made her position any clearer."

This conversation wasn't getting me anywhere. It seems that my counterpart may not have had any information beyond the official statement I already knew by heart. I stood up.

"If there isn't anything more you can tell me, I shouldn't keep you from your work any longer, Mr. Ambassador. Thank you for your time."

Mr. Acting Ambassador stood up as well, expressed once more his profound regrets and handed me a farewell present: a pile of brochures on Iraq. *Iraq: A Traveler's Paradise. Iraq, friend to all people of goodwill. Iraq, the innocent victim of vicious American politics.* Was this guy paid by the number of booklets he could get into circulation?

"My country is a very beautiful, Dr. Hoffmann, and also very hospitable. Perhaps we can welcome you one day to prove that, despite what happened to your friend."

I couldn't imagine any circumstances under which I would put his claim about a beautiful and peace-loving Iraq personally to the test. I nevertheless took his pamphlets with me to avoid appearing impolite. At least I had been spared one of his boss's famous novels.

I had parked my car a block away in front of a church. Only then, as I noticed two elderly women emerging from it, did I realize that it was a Catholic church. A sign identified it as Herz-Jesu-Kirche, "Heart of Jesus Church."

On the spur of the moment, I decided to enter the church. As soon as I stepped inside, I found myself surrounded by a wonderful stillness, a solemn serenity. Two candles were burning at a side altar; they had probably just been lit by the two women I'd seen coming out. I'm a Lutheran and I wasn't even sure whether Celine had been an active Christian in recent years. But I dropped two euros into the small wrought-iron box at the altar and lit a third candle. If there was a God, I wanted him to be gracious to her.

And if there was indeed a God, but he wasn't right there—if, for instance, God was in fact a Buddhist—I was counting on his generosity regarding the limits of human understanding. At the very least, I hoped that he would count the mistake against me and not Celine.

CHAPTER 5

Celine's parents had arranged the funeral entirely on their own, turning down any offers of help from Beate and me.

Their daughter was put to rest at the Zehlendorf Cemetery in Berlin, an attractive spot full of evergreens and colorful annuals. Although Celine's parents had made some concessions in life since their more principled days—like the fact that they were legally married and had made enough money to live in a nice row house in expensive Hamburg—"the Church" was still out of the question. Which was why, although we were on holy ground, a professional funeral orator, not a pastor, shared his thoughts on "taken too early, gone but not forgotten."

The rest of his speech also differed little from what a priest or father would have said. He appeared to believe in some sort of eternal life, but I liked that there was no short—or not-so-short—stopover in hell in his vision. He wasn't very clear on the details, but according to his potpourri of Christian tradition, Hermann Hesse, and indigenous religions, there was definitely a chance of resurrection. He left us to ponder whether our new incarnation would be in the form of a butterfly, an orchid, or a laboratory rat in a pharmaceutical company.

Most of my fellow mourners seemed unperturbed by the inconsistencies of his handcrafted view of the world and eternity. I could tell that many of those in attendance were friends of Celine's parents, not only by their age, but also by their baggy jeans and brightly floral potato-sack dresses. They probably went a long way back, back to the days of anticapitalist kindergartens and antinuke demonstrations. I was waiting for them to suddenly hold hands, form a circle, and start a procession around the grave. Celine would have laughed herself to death.

But Celine was already dead, and the fact that we were standing there was final proof of that.

To the left of me was a group of younger people, most of whom wore business suits or other tailored outfits. Clearly friends of Celine. Some of them I knew well, others I'd only met once or twice, and a few I didn't know at all. I'd always liked that Celine had kept her own circle of friends, that she had not simply merged her life into mine.

That group, which had been informed of the service by Beate, consisted of friends from Celine's high school and university days, and surely a few activists from Pro Asyl. I kept my distance from the latter group. Though I knew it was unfair, I held them at least partially responsible for Celine's fate.

I didn't belong to any group, neither to Celine's friends and colleagues, who were a good ten to fifteen years younger than me, nor to her parents and their friends, who were that much older than me. It was the same old story: too young or too old, too early or too late. Happiness means being in the right place at the right time—at the right age. And the truly happy among us are those who are not overparticular about the exact time, place, or age.

I hadn't gone to the funeral that day to find happiness. But one reason for a funeral service is to help the mourners share the burden of loss, to assure them that they are not alone in their grief. I found, however, that quite the opposite was happening. I felt more desolate and alone than ever.

"Dr. Hoffmann!"

A man who appeared to be somewhere in his fifties, perhaps a bit younger, extended his hand in my direction. He looked Mediterranean, with a full gray beard. I recognized him as Baran, an exiled Kurd from northern Iraq, who had helped Celine learn what was most needed in his homeland, the safest way to get there, and who to contact on arrival. He was the leader of one of several groups of exiled Kurds in Germany. His was the United Democrats of Kurdistan, or something like it.

"We Kurds are very, very sorry about Celine. She was a very good person, always good to us."

Nodding in agreement, a small group of men approached to offer their condolences. Among these people, dressed in their worn but tidy Sunday best, I felt instantly better. I found it strange that I felt bitter about my own countrymen from Pro Asyl, but not about these people, for whom Celine had made this fatal journey.

"Thank you, Baran."

In my pocket, I felt for the key to the basement of the pre-war part of our hospital, which we called "the old building." Even leaving half of the water purification machine behind, Celine and Heiner hadn't had enough space to take everything they had collected for their caravan, and more had kept coming in. Baran was organizing a second transport and needed to get an idea of what had been collected. I handed him the key.

"Any more news from home?"

Baran knew what I meant and shook his head.

"No, not yet. I am sorry. We do not have information about what really happened. But our people are listening. We are sure that what Baghdad says is not true." He pointed toward a small group of younger men farther away. "Those people over there probably know!"

I had thought that the three men he was pointing at were with Baran, but I realized that their suits looked new and tailor-made.

"Saddam Hussein's Secret Service," Baran murmured.

For a moment I was tempted to swoop down on these well-dressed thugs and beat the truth out of them. But I would only have made a fool of myself—and I wouldn't have stood a chance. Besides, unlike Baran, I didn't believe that these field representatives from Iraq had been informed about Celine's true fate. They were probably just pursuing their favorite pastime here: spying on their Kurdish countrymen.

Eventually, the funeral orator had finished with his philosophical meanderings, everyone's hands had been shaken, and all the "I still can't believe its" said. Celine's parents had organized a funeral reception, from which Beate and I had politely excused ourselves. We were quite sure that even the orator would enjoy the meal without us—assuming, of course, that he didn't have to rush off to give some witty speech at some company's anniversary or be the clown at some child's birthday party. Beate gave me a ride home, and we parked in front of my building.

"I'm pretty disappointed," I said.

"Disappointed? What makes you say that?"

"Something doesn't feel right. Like I'm not really mourning."

Beate turned to me. With her bright-blue eyes and long blonde hair, which she wore pinned up, she was at least as pretty as Celine, but in a distinctly different way. Everything about her was somewhat softer, or smoother, than Celine. She reached up to brush an errant strand of hair from her eyes only to have it fall back at once.

"And how does real mourning go, do you think?" she asked.

"I have no idea. Crying fits? Sudden black holes that suck up every thought that isn't about Celine? I feel deserted and disappointed and angry. However, being the conscientious doctor that I am, I just carry on with my same routine."

"You think so? Do you always wear your tie inside out like you did today?"

Beate leaned over and gave me a quick good-bye kiss.

"Will you manage?" she asked.

I nodded at her, only then realizing that we were sitting there holding hands. Had I reached out for Beate's hand, or had she reached out for mine?

General cargo vessel MS *Virgin of the Sea*
Ship owner: Taiwan Trans Global Shipping Company,
Taiwan
Position 53°37´ N / 09°59´ E (Hamburg, Germany)
Loading completed. Crew on board. ETD 11:00 CET.
Port of destination: Karachi, Pakistan

CHAPTER 6

"Good morning. You must be Dr. Hoffmann!"

As I entered my office at the hospital the next morning, an Arabic-looking young man stood up from behind my desk. In his thirties and shamelessly good-looking, he came around the desk and stretched out his hand toward me.

"And who are you?"

"Dr. Hassan, Abdul Hassan. They let you know?"

I ignored his hand and took my seat behind the desk, top-dog style. There were quite a few more patient folders lying there than I had left there the night before.

"No. Nobody told me anything. I have no idea who you are or who gave you the right to come and snoop through our patients' records."

"Well, I am terribly sorry you haven't been informed."

He didn't sound overly sorry to me—more like he didn't think I necessarily deserved to be informed—but at least he had the courtesy to bring me up to date.

"I am a certified doctor in internal medicine from Iraq. I did part of my medical training in Germany, in Cologne. That was years ago. Now I am here on a program run by your GTZ to specialize in nephrology, focusing primarily on different dialysis techniques."

"Who or what is GTZ?"

"The German Agency for Technical Cooperation. It's part of your foreign aid program."

I wasn't too hot on the Iraqis at the moment, and it certainly didn't help when they acted so brazen. He looked to me as though he came from a family within the political establishment. I got our CEO on the phone.

"Oh, Felix, I'm sorry," Beate said. "I forgot to tell you yesterday, you know, with the funeral and all. I haven't even met the man myself yet, but I know that he's a full-fledged internal medicine doctor and that he speaks German fluently. His CV is floating around here somewhere. He's on some program run by our Ministry of Foreign Affairs and isn't costing us a cent! I'm sure he can be of some help, right? Just give him something useful to do. I'll see you later, OK?"

This was not Beate, Celine's and my good friend, speaking. This was Beate, our hospital's CEO. When she was wearing that hat, there was no way she'd pass up a free doctor. And it became my responsibility to make sure that this freebie doctor wouldn't get in our way. I stood up.

"Fine then. Let's head over to the nephrology department so I can introduce you to the staff there." I opened the door. "Incidentally, I would appreciate it if you would only enter my office when I invite you to do so." And I would keep my door locked in the future. No big deal. As soon as Vitalis had found a new department head, I'd have to move out of it anyway.

After delivering our guest to nephrology, I brought myself up to speed on the state of some critical patients while waiting for Professor Kleinweg, our acting chief of internal medicine, to make his weekly appearance. Every Thursday lately, extra care had been given to making the beds, and the patients were anxiously waiting to finally hear a competent opinion. Kleinweg wasn't actually a bad guy, and he didn't go around putting on airs and acting superior. He had enough to deal with at his own hospital and was happy not to be bothered with real medical, let alone administrative, problems at Berlin South. In recent months, we had developed a routine to make his visits pass quickly and smoothly.

Our first patient of the day was Herr Schubert, who had been admitted ten days earlier with a bad asthma attack. Schubert was a routine case. After a week of increased asthma medication and a round of antibiotics, he would be discharged the next day.

When Kleinweg had seen him the week before, he'd told Schubert that he'd been lucky—he'd arrived at the hospital not a moment too soon. So before entering the patient's room, I brought Kleinweg up to date.

"The first bed on your right is Herr Schubert. Acute infectious exacerbation of chronic obstructive pulmonary disease. You saw him last week. Uneventful, discharge tomorrow."

At Schubert's bedside, however, the story sounded a little different.

Me: "You remember Herr Schubert, Herr Professor?"

Kleinweg: "Of course I remember Herr Schubert. Very bad case of chronic asthma with acute infection, touch and go if he would make it. Where is Herr Schubert?"

Kleinweg sounded ready for the worst.

Me: "You are standing right in front of him!"

Kleinweg, looking back and forth between me and the patient, unbelieving: "No! This can't be Herr Schubert!"

Even after Herr Schubert admitted to being Herr Schubert, Kleinweg acted as if he had difficulty believing that this was the same patient who he felt had been doomed to die a week earlier.

"Unbelievable! Excellent work, Dr. Hoffmann."

Once again, a thankful patient would go home and tell his family and friends that the department head himself had confirmed that he had been on the brink of death, and would spread the message that the South Berlin Hospital could work wonders.

Schubert's neighbor in the next bed, a simple case of gastric bleeding from a bit too much aspirin, got Keinweg's same "That was close, not a moment too soon" welcome, along with the assurance that Berlin South would do everything modern medicine had to offer, regardless of cost or trouble, to bring about his recovery. The following week, he would again feign disbelief that the patient had actually survived.

We performed these same theatrics with the other patients. When we visited Herr Krauskopf, the kidney patient, we saw that his temperature had gone down since we had started him on that new aminoglycoside. Kleinweg was hopeful, he told the patient. Mrs. Zachels was also pleased, as the gynecologists had somehow stopped her uterine myoma from bleeding and her angina was better. Herr Schlups wanted to know whether he could still go bowling with a pacemaker.

"You bet, Herr Schlups. You'll do even better than before," Kleinweg assured him.

Of course, Herr Schlups, who still hadn't signed the informed consent form for the implant, had repeatedly asked me and the younger residents the same question—and gotten the exact same answer. But once the professor had spoken, Herr Schlups finally signed the form.

Our last patient, Herr Cornelsen, was the real problem. But his issue wasn't primarily medical, nor could it be solved with our acting routine.

"Your Herr Cornelsen still hasn't been discharged?" he asked.

It sounded less like a reproach than a hope that I was mistaken.

"No, sorry. This time some kind of throat infection cropped up."

Herr Cornelsen had been a diabetic for years. Meanwhile he was not only insulin-dependent but also dialysis-dependent, which meant he'd be hooked up to the kidney machine for hours three times a week. Initially he had only been admitted to optimize his insulin regimen. That had been a matter of a few days, but then, each time he was about to be discharged, he developed some new problem, generally an infection of some kind. He not only blocked one of our precious dialysis machines three times a week, but also required expensive antibiotics. His treatment costs had reached well above what his compulsory health insurance would reimburse the hospital. It was time for my usual Thursday joke.

"Doesn't *your* hospital specialize in diabetes, Herr Professor?"

At this, Kleinweg hastily bid us farewell and he'd remain out of reach again for another week.

It wasn't time for lunch quite yet, so I stopped by the surgery department. Businessman Sommer had kept his word. Operating theaters two and three actually had compressed air coming out of the ports labeled "compressed air," and the distilled water no longer scalded your fingers.

"We're ready for your kidney, Felix!"

Good to know, but I staved the surgeons off for the time being.

I joined Beate for lunch once or twice a week, thereby saving us both time and allowing us to be more informal than if I'd made an appointment with her through her secretary. As far as I was concerned, the matter of Dr. Hassan wasn't quite resolved. Beate apologized again, she herself having only been informed of his arrival only a couple of days earlier by the city health department.

"That happened astonishingly fast, considering the normal pace of our city bureaucrats," I said.

"Can't you just be happy when they make things happen quickly for once? I think the decision came directly from the

Ministry of Foreign Affairs, which certainly would have sped things up a bit. Maybe it's a way of compensating Iraq for the fact that we canceled that delegation of business VIPs from Germany. When it comes to German industry, it seems we'll do business with anyone, even Saddam Hussein himself."

That's globalization for you. Everything is interdependent these days, even the staffing of Berlin South and German foreign policy!

"At least he speaks German, which is becoming increasingly rare around here. In gynecology, you can't find your way to the bathroom without knowing some Russian."

"Are you becoming racist, Felix? Don't forget that at least a third of our patients aren't native Germans. It's not only fair to have foreign doctors on staff but also useful, don't you think?"

I had to agree. I just wished *I* could understand them.

"Moreover," Beate continued, reaching her hand across the table and placing it on mine, "helping Iraq train its doctors means we're actively helping people there, something Celine would have certainly subscribed to."

"Celine was thinking of the Kurds."

"Nonsense. Celine cared about *all* people. Should all Iraqis be made to suffer because of their mad dictator?"

I felt that tightness in my throat again. This was one of the conversations I used to have with Celine, who also usually had the more persuasive argument.

"Of course not. I just fear that neither the Kurds nor the Iraqis will benefit from the advanced qualifications Dr. Hassan will acquire from working here. At the end of the day, he'll either return to his fancy home in Baghdad, where he'll be accessible only to the financial elite, or stay here. Maybe he'll help Saddam with his WMD program."

"That's what he'll be learning in your internal medicine department?"

Beate scored the last point, which meant I let her clear her dishes herself. At times I can be pretty ungentlemanlike.

From: Berlin Station
To: CIA Headquarters, Langley, Virginia
Subject: Dr. Felix Hoffmann
Source: Video surveillance and [blackened out]

Dr. Felix Hoffmann entered the embassy of the Republic of Iraq in Berlin-Zehlendorf at 09:14. According to [blackened out], Hoffmann met with acting ambassador Nasif Hamdai. It is assumed that Mr. Hamdai heads and coordinates Iraqi intelligence in Western Europe. The subject matter of their discussion is not yet known. Hoffmann left the embassy at 09:46 holding papers he had not entered with. The subject matter of these papers is not known. Appraisal: Cooperation of Felix Hoffmann and Celine Bergkamp with Iraqi authorities, especially Iraqi intelligence, has long been suspected. This meeting further substantiates that theory, as well as our belief that the so-called "humanitarian help" transported by Ms. Bergkamp happened in close cooperation with Iraqi authorities. Suggested further action: Continuous surveillance of Dr. Hoffmann is strongly recommended. Sharing findings with German Intelligence is not recommended.

Addendum: video surveillance of Iraqi embassy Berlin 09:12–09:14 and 09:46–09:48.

Handwritten addendum: Continuous surveillance of Dr. Hoffmann not possible due to staff shortage.

CHAPTER 7

Berlin South again had to get along without me the next morning. The indispensable Dr. Hoffmann had to accept the invitation of his esteemed former colleague Dr. Zentis to the "first workshop on restructuring civil protection and disaster management" at Berlin's health department.

I left home early that morning. Since I had to go downtown anyway, I planned to pay another visit to our ministry of foreign affairs on the way. Trying to reach them by phone had proved to an aggravating task. First of all, they are not listed among the "Ministries of the Federal Republic of Germany" in the phone book. After some deep thinking, I realized that has some logic to it, because they don't call themselves the "Ministry of Foreign Affairs" but rather the "Foreign Office."

And indeed, that is how I finally hunted up their telephone number. When I dialed the number, an automated voice told me to please hold and that the next available operator would be all mine. While waiting, I was entertained with country music. But by the time I remembered the name of the song and wondered if the music ever changes with our international interests, I was suddenly disconnected.

This was not my first time at 1 Werderscher Markt, the address of our ministry of foreign affairs, since Celine had disappeared. The doorman knew me at that point and quickly got on the phone to announce my visit to Under-undersecretary Schmockwitz. I think I owed it to the doorman and his persistence that the under-undersecretary would see me without an appointment. "You know your way, right? And Dr. Hoffmann, I am very sorry about what happened to your friend."

The doorman's expression of sympathy sounded more sincere than Under-undersecretary Schmockwitz's condolences once I had taken a seat in his plush third-floor office overlooking the Spree River and the Berlin Cathedral.

"Thank you for your sympathy, Herr Schmockwitz. Of course the reason I am here today is to inquire whether the investigation has turned up anything new."

The under-undersecretary raised his shoulders in a shrug.

"Our crisis management group has given the case a great deal of attention, believe me. But it might be years before we know definitively what happened—for instance, whether the Iraqis told us the truth."

"The Iraqis are not telling you the truth. How often do you need me to explain that to you?"

"Yes, you have said as much. But the fact is, with the repatriation of the body, the case is no longer a priority for us, at least for the time being. However much I personally regret this."

I got up. "If the case is no longer a priority, I don't understand why the security people are harassing me and snooping into Ms. Bergkamp's past!"

I stood up and walked out, slamming the door behind me. I hoped I wouldn't need this Schmockwitz for any reason ever again.

At the bottom of my bourgeois heart, I am a law-abiding citizen who tries to follow the rules. So I was happy that, even with my stop at the Foreign Office, I was still five minutes early when I parked my car in the health department's underground garage. "Task force Dr. Zentis/Undersecretary Mueller: Conference Room 5, 2nd floor" a sign in the lobby informed me. Second floor meant that at least I didn't have to entrust myself to the elevators.

Since this was going to be about disaster management, most hospitals had sent their head ER doctors, including my colleague from the Charité University Hospital.

"What kind of workshop is this? There isn't a bite of food, not even a veggie platter!"

He wasn't the only one disappointed. Hospital doctors are always about to perish from hunger. I wondered whether other professions also constantly face acute starvation.

After Undersecretary Mueller gave a short welcome and introduction, Dr. Zentis took over and ran the rest of the show. Zentis didn't pass up the chance to underscore both his own personal importance and the importance of the subject. He had thoroughly analyzed—and captured on PowerPoint—the current contingency plans ("Pitiful!") and what we would surely be up against ("If not even worse!") in the future ("If not even sooner!"). I catnapped through most of his presentation since I had spent a pleasant evening going through the materials he had sent out in advance. But I didn't hold this repetition against him. I knew that at least half of my medical colleagues didn't read anything longer than a patient information leaflet, if even that much.

"So far we've managed every situation that's come up, Zentis," said Dr. Vogel, the head of Berlin South's ER department, who I had brought along for support. He too remembered the La Belle bombing. "Over two hundred people injured, all emergencies treated on the spot, and at a hospital in no time. We don't have skyscrapers like the Twin Towers in Berlin, do we?"

Dr. Zentis and Undersecretary Mueller were far from ready to have their project fall to pieces.

"We are thinking of scenarios, even here in Berlin, that would make you wish you'd been in New York on 9/11."

It suddenly became clear what was coming next. We were there to learn about a planned antiterrorism field exercise we would be part of. Current chains of communications, availability of response teams, and means of medical treatment would all be put to the test. Everybody at the workshop was assigned a role, and there was no chance to duck away. I was assigned the role of disaster coordinator for the Berlin urban districts of Charlottenburg-Wilmersdorf and Steglitz-Zehlendorf, which pretty much corresponded to our hospital's draw area anyway. It could have been worse. But my mind was elsewhere. I had to decide what to cook for Beate on Sunday night. And make a list of what I needed to buy.

CHAPTER 8

For dinner with Beate, I fell back on one of my tried-and-true recipes: pork medallions on green beans, cherry tomatoes, and onions, prepared au gratin with Roquefort cheese. It was one of my standards because it was hard to mess up. I didn't question too deeply why I felt this way, but I wanted my dinner with Beate to turn out just right.

"This is wonderful! Is there more of it?"

Since Germans lack the good manners of Americans, who will compliment you on your cooking even when they hate it, I could take Beate's compliment at face value. Which made me feel good. Beate wore her blonde hair down, and a dress just long enough to be appropriate for her age. She had brought the wine, and with it an air of early spring. Celine had never used perfume. She had referred to it as "commercialized femininity" and said it reminded her of animal testing in the cosmetics industry. The fact was, Celine hadn't needed any makeup or perfume. Nor did Beate, actually, but even with it, she still looked good.

So far, we had largely focused on dinner, but it was time for a little pause. It occurred to me that I had only ever been alone with Beate in her capacity as CEO. So there was a lot I didn't know about her, like, for example, whether she'd had to cancel some other date to have dinner with Dr. Hoffmann.

"Felix, are you asking about my love life?"

"Well, now that you mention it…"

"You know, of course, that at our age, everybody's in some kind of relationship, more or less…"

"And how is yours? More or less?"

Beate shrugged her bare shoulders.

"Whatever—it's nothing like you and Celine had."

Which was precisely what I had been pondering the last few weeks: What exactly was it that Celine and I had? We had clicked, almost at first sight, that was true. But what had come after that? Was she the woman I had always dreamed of? Had we in fact been the dream team most people saw us to be? Or had we just been very good friends with benefits?

"Perhaps we just got used to each other after all that time."

"That too, Felix, of course. How else could you have been together for so long? But one thing is for sure: Celine loved you, very much so."

Celine had never told me as much, but then neither had I. And now I never could.

"What else did she tell you about us?"

"Like what?"

"C'mon on, Beate. You women talk about these things."

Beate helped herself to another serving of pork, then gave me an innocent look.

"You mean, what she liked most about you? What made her furious? Or"—with a mischievous look—"if you were any good?"

Was that what I had meant? Not really, but it was an interesting question.

"And—was I?"

Innocent look again.

"Fair to average, I heard."

Served me right. After all, I had asked. I couldn't make it any worse, so I pressed the issue.

"And—did she have a qualified basis to compare to?"

Beate put her fork and knife down on her newly empty plate and leaned back comfortably in her chair.

"Any dessert?"

After fresh figs with pink peppercorns, Beate kicked off her flats and flopped onto my couch, tired and full. As I went to the kitchen to make two strong espressos, I realized it was probably just as well that my last question had gone unanswered. Eager not to constrict each other's freedom, Celine and I had what you would call an open relationship. But everybody knows what happens when one partner acts on that option.

"So how about you, Felix? Have you always been faithful?"

I took off my shoes and sat down next to Beate.

"What do you mean? Physically or mentally?"

Beate pressed her big toe into my stomach.

"That is semantics, Felix!"

Before I could respond, the doorbell rang. I opened the door to discover Celine's parents standing there.

"Sorry, we don't want to intrude. We didn't know you had company."

"You're not intruding. What can I do for you?"

They repeated that they didn't want to disturb me, that they just wanted to give me the key to Celine's apartment and wondered if I could check on the place from time to time.

"Her apartment...But I have a key...You don't want to... Please, come in, first of all."

They kept their position in front of my door and pointedly avoided looking over my shoulder.

"Thank you, but we're taking the first flight home tomorrow morning. Have a good night."

They handed me the key and were gone. I felt bad. I may not have been on the best terms with Celine's parents, but I felt sorry for them, of course. I knew that Celine's room was still waiting for her in their Hamburg row house. A room with much more to remind them of her daughter than the apartment across the street from me: books from her high school days, her first high heels perhaps, her favorite doll. I heard a taxi's diesel engine come to a stop outside, car doors opening and shutting, and the car taking off.

By the time I turned around, Beate had put her shoes back on and was standing right behind me. She thanked me for the evening with a light kiss on the cheek.

"See you tomorrow."

Then she was gone, too.

Maybe, I thought, it was a good thing that Celine's parents had shown up when they did. Would our comforting each other have gotten out of hand otherwise? Or had I actually planned on it when I issued my invitation to Beate? Had I been ready to be unfaithful to Celine? Could you even be unfaithful to somebody who was dead? Again, I decided not to ponder the matter too deeply. I told myself that it was a good chance to go to bed early and get the workweek off to a brisk start. Not a bad idea since I would be on call on Monday night.

CHAPTER 9

That was one of the major disadvantages of our clinic's current structure. Apart from the Thursday morning procession with Professor Kleinweg, I had the honor of exercising all the functions of a department head, but I enjoyed none of the privileges. At least not the privilege of spending every night in my own bed at home. Due to our staffing shortage, I still had to be on night duty at least once a week. So first thing on Monday I arrived at the hospital in a preventative bad mood, only to be proven right that night. I was running around until dawn, not only saving lives but also seeing patients who hadn't found the time to see their GP about their headache/rash/diarrhea during the day or who in the middle of the night urgently needed a second opinion. Things never quieted down long enough for me to sit down, let alone sleep.

And there was no chance on Tuesday to make up for the ugly night and abscond a little early. It was the first Tuesday of the month, which meant we had a budget conference. If I skipped it, my colleagues in the other departments would happily slash the last aspirin allotted to internal medicine.

By six p.m., I had ensured that my department wouldn't have to cut back on medication or lab time more than any of the others, and I started out for home. On my way to the parking lot, I saw more people piling up at the emergency desk than was typical for a Tuesday night. Which was OK with me, because we had in fact freed up some beds earlier. Plus it wasn't my problem anymore. My only business at the moment was getting home, having a beer, and falling into bed.

The first call came around seven thirty p.m. I had just dozed off on the couch, and my answer was as friendly as you'd expect under the circumstances.

"Doctor," I snarled into the phone. "If you can't handle the situation yourself, call your backup. And if you can't reach your backup, call in any one of your colleagues who is stupid enough to pick up the phone."

Twenty minutes later, I was just trying to get back to sleep, with the help of a second beer, when my colleague Valenta called.

"Felix, I'm afraid you have to come back in. Something strange is going on here."

"What's the problem?"

"Can't talk about it over the phone. Just get your pretty ass in here ASAP!"

Heinz Valenta headed our ICU and had been a doctor for about as long as I had. He wouldn't call me without a good reason. But then, why was he being so secretive? With a hearty yawn, I put the unfinished beer down on the table and started searching for my car keys.

The hospital's emergency department looked like an overcrowded field hospital. People everywhere were sniffling and coughing. Face masks were being passed out as fast as possible. Valenta came up to me, mask over his mouth and nose, and handed me one, too.

"What's happening here, Heinz? Our dear GPs can't treat a cold anymore?"

"That's part of the problem. Most of these patients were in fact referred to us by their GPs. But rightly so, I think."

Several of my residents were running around with rather alarmed looks on their faces. As I reviewed their notes, I began to understand why Valenta had called me in. There was a pattern. Our coughers and snifflers had all been at a pop concert at the O2 arena two days before and had all begun to feel sick two mornings later: thoracic pain, fever, sore throat. Some of them were even coughing up blood.

Valenta looked at me.

"No good, right?"

"No, no good at all."

"I already alerted the epidemics people over at the Robert Koch Institute."

"What did they say?"

"Put them all into isolation."

"Great idea! Would have never occurred to us. Did they happen to tell you where to find the space for that?"

Valenta gave me a smile.

"That's why I called you. You're acting department head, remember?"

No doctor trusts his colleagues completely. Because of that— and to buy myself some time—I put on the face mask and started to interview some of the patients myself. I always got the same answer: they'd been to the concert two days before and were sick today. Cough, sniffle, cough, cough.

I made the third patient tell me his story twice, and then I went looking for Valenta. I found him talking on two phone lines at the same time.

"Say, Heinz, have you talked to any of these patients yourself?"

"No time to, just trying to control the chaos." He yelled some-thing into the phone, and then slammed it down. "Our micro-biologists probably don't even know how to get here at night. They've never had to!"

"Do me a favor, Heinz. Talk to some of these patients yourself, will you? I'll get the microbiologists moving in the meantime."

Which I actually did not do. By then, I was pretty sure foul play was afoot. I waited for Valenta to finish his interviews.

"Rather a lot of conformity in these histories, don't you think?" I said.

"Yep. Reminds me of an article I read about a class whose students all downloaded the same essay from the Internet. And the coughing is a little too pronounced."

To be on the safe side, I called the ER at the Spree Hospital.

"Epidemic? Not in this part of town. Just our usual alcoholics and shot wounds."

Valenta had overheard my conversation.

"That's just because of our amazing reputation. When the plague breaks out in this city, Berlin South is the place to go!"

That was the last of Valenta's humor for the night. Judging by the color of his face, his normal blood pressure of 160 had prob-ably reached a good 200 by then.

"Felix, why don't you go for a little walk. In fact, take your resi-dents along with you. Meanwhile, I'll find out who's behind all this."

Valenta weighed well over 200 pounds—and each one of them was in a rage at this point. I had a sense of foreboding about what might happen to our coughers if Valenta stayed on. I put my hand on his shoulder.

"*You* go for a walk, Heinz. Better still, go and send our micro-biologists home. Meanwhile, I'm going to give a good friend of mine a call."

I called the number I had been given a few days before.

"Operations center. Please identify yourself."

"This is Dr. Hoffmann, South Berlin Hospital. I need to speak to Dr. Zentis. Pronto!"

It only took a few seconds.

"Dr. Zentis speaking."

Of course he'd been told who was calling. I could even see his stupid grin through the phone.

"Listen, Zentis. We're running a hospital here, if you even remember what that is after all your years working in the health bureaucracy. A hospital, not a circus."

Zentis, remaining calm, answered earnestly.

"A number of as yet unidentified individuals, probably Arab terrorists, sprayed an aerosol containing *Yersinia pestis* at a pop concert at the O2 arena the day before yesterday. Earlier this evening, we were made aware of the developing situation, which is most serious indeed."

I was at a loss. Zentis sounded dead serious. And I had just sent our microbiologists home! But then I remembered the good old times.

"Zentis, you sound very persuasive, I'll admit that much. But you were always an excellent liar. Especially when something went wrong with a patient of yours. Don't tell me you even knew how to spell *Yersinia pestis* a few weeks ago. If the plague had really landed in Berlin, not even your friends at the health department would have made you—of all people—Berlin's pest doctor. Whatever kind of doctor you think you are, you are neither a specialist in infectious disease nor a microbiologist."

Did I really believe that? Hadn't I personally witnessed how the undersecretary had been hanging on Zentis's every word? How would the bureaucrats ever find out he was a charlatan and a show-off?

"Herr Hoffmann, it is time you set aside your personal feelings. Exercise PP, which stands for 'pneumonic plague,' was begun this afternoon at seventeen hundred hours. The patients coughing at your hospital will be taking notes: How long did it take for a doctor to see them? When were they provided with a face mask? When and how effectively were they isolated? We will then analyze their notes and other data to find out, among other things, how your department has performed."

By then my blood pressure must have been somewhere up near Valenta's level.

"Do you have any idea what your stupid theatrics mean to real emergency patients here, Zentis? How many truly sick people we didn't see and treat in time tonight? I just hope your clowns are also taking notes on that—and that you've paid your liability insurance."

But Dr. Zentis wasn't the type to be easily intimidated. Taking responsibility for his mistakes wasn't his thing.

"Do you really think, Herr Hoffmann, that in the case of a terrorist attack our hospitals wouldn't still have to treat their other emergency patients as well? Like I said, the exercise has begun. As you know, you are the responsible medical supervisor for the Berlin districts of Charlottenburg-Wilmersdorf and Steglitz-Zehlendorf. Which is why you should get over here at once and start doing your job."

Sure. After the last thirty-six hours, what could be more fun than playing plague epidemic in the sandbox with old Zentis! But if I wanted to keep Berlin South out of the line of fire, friendly or unfriendly—and out of sight of the hatchet men in the health department—I had no choice but to follow his call to the war room. He'd clearly won the first round.

CHAPTER 10

As it turned out, I actually enjoyed my days working on the plague exercise. It made for a nice change from the day-to-day routine in the hospital and kept me so busy that I didn't have time to think all the time about Celine and why she'd had to die. Plus it was fun to move all the available ambulances, police officers and firefighters around on the city map, close down the Zoo train station for all but local trains, and shut down all the restaurants and movie theaters in my districts. While I was doing that, I kept an eye on Zentis, waiting for him to make a mistake. But he had been planning this exercise for a long time and seemed well prepared.

At the end of day one, we counted 1,174 infections and 186 deaths from pulmonary plague. Day two saw 2,807 infected and almost 500 deaths, and we were running out of respirators in Berlin. By the end of day three, we were faced with 5,556 infections and 1,424 deaths.

At Berlin South, I had made visiting doctor Hassan the in-house coordinator for the exercise, so that none of our regular residents would be tied up by this rigmarole.

In Zentis's war room, we didn't only have medical problems to deal with. Every department involved—and that was almost everybody, from the police force to the undertakers—wanted to have a say, which meant more time spent in meetings every day. Zentis even wanted to call in the army to control panic and looting.

"Good idea," I said. "I'll dedicate enough antibiotics to keep the firing squads alive."

We did in fact start to run short of antibiotics. So one of the important questions became who should be treated prophylactically: Only the people who had been in direct contact with an infected individual? All potential emergency responders? The families of emergency responders? And how large an area should we quarantine?

On the evening of day three, I went home. I had spent the last few nights on a cot in the cellar of the health department and was yearning for a private shower and my own bed. On top of that, I couldn't have stood Zentis another minute. Nevertheless, after a relaxing glass of wine, I checked my newly created e-mail account hoffmann@pp-exercise.de, for the latest developments. As I'd expected, Zentis hadn't been idle. I read his new order, laughed out loud, and still laughing, crawled into bed.

The telephone woke me up at six o'clock the next morning, half an hour later than I'd expected. I just let it ring while I got the coffee machine going. Five minutes later it rang again. It was my friend Zentis, of course.

"Herr Hoffmann. Exercise PP is still running. You have left the war room without permission!"

"You're right. So now what? Are you going to have me shot?"

"We've got no time for your adolescent antics. The morning conference will be at seven thirty sharp!"

"I'm terribly sorry, Zentis, but it looks like you'll have to get along without me. Last night at eight thirteen, you put all of Berlin under quarantine, remember? Me, too."

That left him speechless, but only for a moment.

"Had you been here, in your assigned position, you would have received a badge last night like everybody else on the team, allowing you to move around freely. I'll send a police car to pick you up."

"That won't work either, dear Zentis. Take a look at the gas situation in Berlin. There's been a lot of panic buying, with everyone trying to get away from the plague. It's true that's taken care of now; nobody's getting out now with that quarantine of yours. But remember: no gas is getting into the city either. Even if you badge the drivers, you won't persuade them to drive their tankers into plague-ridden Berlin. How is it that the phones are still working anyway? People at the power plants are still working? How did they get to work?"

There was another pause on the other end of the line, but only a short one.

"That is precisely why we're running this exercise. To be prepared for any eventuality, not only to find out that we have inadequate supplies of antibiotics, but also to show people that it was a mistake to liquidate our stockpile of gas and coal and everything else the city had set aside during the Cold War."

Zentis hung up. I had to concede that he wasn't all wrong. But I'd learned by then that all Zentis had done was copy a bioterrorism exercise staged in Denver, Colorado, in May 2000. He had even used the same infectious agent, *Yersinia pestis*. Berlin could have saved a lot of time and money just by simply studying the results from Denver. But that would have deprived Zentis of the chance to show us all how important he was. We had learned one thing: his quarantine had come too late. That morning, his war room announced the first cases of plague in other parts of Germany.

CHAPTER 11

I treated myself to another espresso before driving to the hospital. It was Saturday morning, which not only reminded me of all the breakfasts I'd enjoyed with Celine but also made me realize how much of a sacrifice she'd made by agreeing to have breakfast with me every Saturday morning at eight o'clock. Because, unlike me, Celine actually loved to sleep in.

Berlin South had come through the virtual attack of the plague bacteria all right. In my office, though, the consequences of my having been away for three days covered almost the entire desk. I decided that the letters, having waited so long for an answer, could wait a little longer. Like the one from some GP asking how on earth we thought he could continue the kind of treatment we had initiated on his patient with the budget he had to work with. And the one from some alternative healer, who demanded to know how we had dared to discontinue his combined magnetic/ Bach flower therapy, thus putting his patient's life at risk.

Saturday morning was a good time to meet with patients. On Sundays they were usually with family, dining in a nearby restaurant or strolling around our park. When I wanted to see them on weekdays, they had often disappeared with a colleague from another medical specialty—off to the X-ray department or doing a test somewhere in the labyrinth of the hospital. But that Saturday I had the opportunity to meet with almost all of them and I confirmed that they had survived my absence. I wasn't indispensable after all!

I found our visiting doctor from Iraq in the nephrology office, brooding over a pile of computer printouts.

"Herr Hassan! You too are spending your Saturday at the hospital? What's all this paper?"

"I still have to work on some data from our virtual plague patients. It's a good time to do it, since the patients on dialysis at the moment are doing fine."

Judging from what I'd seen from Zentis's war room, the plague experiment had run smoothly at Berlin South under Dr. Hassan's leadership. To make up for having misjudged him, I complimented him on a job well done.

"You've done a fine job here with the plague experiment. Thank you very much."

"Thank you, Herr Hoffmann. But then, I had a head start. Back home we constantly train for situations like that: poison gas attacks, infectious agents, anything we might be up against from the Americans."

From the Americans? More likely for protection from the fallout of something Saddam's army might like to deploy. But I kept my thoughts to myself. After all, Dr. Hassan was our guest.

"Whatever. Good work! One thing in particular surprised me: How come we were the only hospital that didn't run out of respirators on day two? Did you cheat on the numbers there?"

"No, no cheating." Dr. Hassan laughed. "I simply reactivated the decommissioned ones that were in the basement of the old building. On paper, that is."

That was clever. But I also found it interesting how quickly our guest had learned his way around our hospital.

"Those respirators are waiting to be shipped to Iraq, the northern parts mainly. You've probably heard about it. If we'd had enough space on the trucks the first time around, those machines would be up and running there now, as would a mobile water purification plant."

Hassan put the computer printouts aside.

"Yes, so I've heard. Your colleagues also told me about your friend. I am very sorry, especially since she wanted to help my country."

"Well, you probably heard that the help was for the Kurds in your country."

"Yes, I know. That is the problem. We regard the Kurds as citizens of Iraq. But that is not how the Kurds see it."

Again I had to stop myself from making a snide remark, like that it might be difficult for them to regard themselves as citizens of a country whose army shoots mustard gas at them.

"In any event," I said instead, "I can assure you that my friend would never have exploded a bomb in your country. Or anywhere else."

Hassan simply shrugged.

"You must understand," he said, "the whole world is conspiring against Iraq, which inevitably leads to some paranoia. My family is not part of the Saddam clan, we come from another part of the country. But we have connections. If you'd like, I can ask my family to make a few inquiries."

I gladly accepted his offer. Hassan asked me for a few details, including the route Celine had taken, the names of her contacts in Iraq, and how we had communicated. I was happy to give him the information, and hoped that I would get further than I had with Baran and his United Democrats of Kurdistan, from whom I hadn't heard a word since Celine's burial.

I thanked Hassan once more and left him to finish with his printouts. The next person I wanted to talk to was Beate, who I was sure I would also find somewhere around the hospital on a Saturday morning. I paged her, and she told me to come over to surgery, where Herr Sommer's men had finally finished chiseling the walls and plastering them again. She was looking on as our surgeons and our in-house technician, Willi, checked the new installations.

"Hello, here I am, back from a most important government assignment I'm not allowed to talk about. Did my job fall victim to some new streamlining of personnel?

"No such luck, Felix." Beate put her hand on my shoulder. "You're still part of the treadmill. And if you didn't pee on some undersecretary's desk while on your secret plague mission, your old job might even still be yours."

I hadn't peed on anybody's desk. But I had left the exercise early and without permission, and I had questioned Zentis's decisions—which was probably an even greater sin against the health department.

"Speaking of my job, Beate, anything in the grapevine about the new internal medicine department head?"

"From what I hear, they've agreed on three candidates they want to interview."

Beate took me aside. Of course she knew that I had applied for the job. And both of us knew that my chances were slim. The problem was, they were looking for a team player. Though I considered myself to be one, my team was Berlin South. For the Vitalis group, however, the team was all of their holdings. But there was something else Beate wanted to tell me.

"Baran called me."

Just a few minutes earlier, I had complained to myself that he hadn't called me. But of course, his primary contact had been Celine, and became, naturally, Beate.

"So—has he found out anything?" My hopes were rising. After all, the UDK was the biggest of the many Kurdish organizations in Germany.

"Well, yes."

There was some hesitation in Beate's voice.

"C'mon, Beate. What did Baran have to say?"

"Well, nothing definite. But there are murmurs among the Kurds in Iraq that Celine's shipment wasn't 'clean.'"

"Not clean? Meaning what?"

"Baran himself isn't sure yet but he's keeping his ears open."

Had my two visitors from homeland security been right? Had Celine and Heiner really picked up weapons or some kind of explosive somewhere in Eastern Europe? Perhaps without knowing they had done so? Or maybe Heiner knew, but not Celine? Had that stuff she didn't know about blown up on her at some point? Was what the Iraqis were claiming true, at least in part? Beate and I both were at a loss.

I retreated to my office and went to work on that pile of paper that had accumulated on my desk. Angry and frustrated, I blanked out all thought so effectively that by that evening I had taken care of every single query and complaint. A whole Sunday lay ahead of me like a black hole. I called Beate, who was also still in her office. Would she, quid pro quo, like to cook for me the next night?

"I don't know, Felix…"

"What do you mean 'I don't know'?" It occurred to me again how little I knew about Beate's private life. "You said yourself you were a better cook than Celine!"

I heard a short laugh over the phone.

"And as I added, that wasn't saying much." There was a moment of silence as she mulled over my suggestion. "OK, listen. Let's meet for dinner tomorrow. But not at my place or yours."

"Neutral territory?"

No answer.

"I think you're just too lazy to cook!" I said.

We finally decided to meet at Luigi's.

"The food is good there and we'll be doing something to foster German-Italian relations," I said.

Beate agreed.

General cargo vessel MS *Virgin of the Sea*
Position 14°34´ N / 19°53´ E (150 nautical miles
west of Dakar)
Overflight satellite DSP 22 (type keyhole 11) calculated for 22:13:06 UT. All engines shut down
from 18:00 UT to 22:30 UT. All lights off from
22:00 UT to 22:30 UT.

CHAPTER 12

Luigi, proprietor and chef of the *ristorante* he'd named after himself, had been Celine's greatest fan after me. At times even ahead of me. When I showed up with Beate, he openly demonstrated his disapproval. But he made no mention of Celine until I told him what had happened, or rather, what I'd been told had happened.

"*Signorina Celine e una bomba? Assolutamente impossibile!*"

"By the way, you've met Beate. She was Celine's best friend," I said, introducing Beate to him.

"*Ma certo!* How could I forget!"

Slapping his forehead in recognition, he appeared genuinely relieved, and right away he absorbed Beate into his spacious Italian heart.

Which I could understand. Beate had again cooperated with the cosmetics industry, and the result made it hard to hold anything against this branch of the economy. Had they added pheromones to her perfume? I was wondering whether she could tell how much her "not at my place or yours" conflicted with the kind of explosive femininity she was presenting. Her insistence on "neutral territory" instantly seemed more than reasonable. In

any case, we spent an agreeable night at Luigi's, and this time I got
my quick good-night kiss on the mouth.

"So where do we go from here?"

OK, Hoffmann. What did she mean by that? I'd studied some psy-
chology back in med school and it was part of my daily job. Was
Beate testing me? Or was I missing a chance if I played it safe? I
decided to play it safe and waited for her to continue, which she
did.

"Seems to me we need more information, more reliable information that is."

You can say that again, I thought to myself. But it was becom-
ing clear to me what she was referring to, so I made a suggestion:
"Maybe Baran has heard something. Or our visiting doctor from
Iraq. He promised to ask his family to look into Celine's fate."

The other matter remained unresolved, that night and at my
next dinner with Beate, once again at my place. I served gilthead
sea bream with grilled tomatoes and fresh herbs, and the evening
went pretty much the way my other meals with Beate had gone.
Perhaps her goodnight-kiss had a little more intensity this time?
Was I reading her signals correctly, or weren't there even any?
Was she just a very attractive woman who enjoyed talking to me?
Or had I become her social project of the month, a man in need
of a little motherly sympathy? I dismissed that possibility at once.

Beate's early departure gave me time to browse the
"Preliminary Report on an Assumed Terrorist Attack with *Yersinia
pestis* in Berlin," which had just arrived by e-mail. Although the
document was described as preliminary, I was surprised at how
quickly Zentis had pulled the data together.

More than that, though, I was irritated by the fact that Zentis
was calling for a conference to discuss and adopt his report as
early as the following afternoon, as I hoped that, unlike me, my

former colleagues on the plague team had better ways to spend their Sunday night than studying Zentis's report. I printed out the eighty-page document, helped myself to the rest of the chardonnay, and started reading.

"Hide it in the middle" is a tried-and-true method that involves burying weak statistics or findings that don't add up deep in the middle of a scientific paper. And that was exactly where I found what the hasty Sunday-night reader probably wasn't supposed to discover, in the tables showing the estimated infections and deaths subdivided by district and the different hospitals involved.

It was so typical of Zentis! The urban districts and hospitals for which he'd been directly responsible had only about half the infections relative to their population, hardly any secondary infections, and significantly fewer fatalities. No explanation for this interesting aberration could be found in any of the numerous tables. Apparently Zentis's population miraculously enjoyed far better immunity than the rest of the city. I thought of another reason why Zentis had come up with these impressive figures for the areas under his jurisdiction and finally went to bed with a nasty grin on my face. The press conference would be interesting indeed.

Just as I was about to fall asleep, the phone rang. It was Beate.

"I just wanted to say good night."

"Thanks, Beate. You sleep well, too."

CHAPTER 13

There are certainly plenty of differences between hospitals run by the public health service and those managed by a for-profit organization, but they also have a few things in common, one of which is that no one ever passes up a glass of champagne. In this case, it was to honor the official approval of the newly installed purified water, gas, and compressed-air systems in the surgery department. The champagne had been provided by industrialist Sommer himself, who personally attended the occasion. Surely this €1.5 million project was nothing exceptional for his company, but again, he surely hoped there was more to come.

"Plus," Valenta commented, with a bottle of champagne in one hand and a plate overloaded with canapés in the other, "this is a unique opportunity for Herr Sommer to see all of Vitalis's decision makers at once—there's a lot to be done in their other hospitals."

"Yes, I sure hope so!"

Herr Sommer, who was suddenly standing beside us with his glass of champagne, had evidently overheard the last part of our conversation.

"Which is precisely why I wanted to bribe you with a nice dinner, Dr. Hoffmann. Are you free tonight?"

Dinner invitations from industrialist Sommer have the distinction of being both a way of getting to know the hippest swank restaurants in Berlin and of adding up to a bill that could be construed as bribery.

"I think you overestimate my influence within the Vitalis Group, Herr Sommer. Times are changing, and soon I'll be back to being just an ordinary senior resident." I pointed in the direction of the men standing around the buffet. "You should really be making dinner dates with Herr Hirth and his top managers over there."

Sommer laughed.

"Don't worry, Dr. Hoffmann, I did. But don't underestimate your reputation within the Vitalis Group."

Was that true? Did Sommer know more than I did? Like some information regarding who might become the new department head? So I said I'd be happy to meet him for dinner that night. I just hoped that the conference with Zentis that afternoon wouldn't spoil my appetite.

Two hours later, I found myself back in Conference Room 5. No champagne there. Even so, Zentis was in good spirits.

"The aim of the exercise, dear colleagues—which was to determine the state of emergency-and-catastrophe planning for Berlin and any potential flaws in those plans—has been more than fulfilled, and I want to thank you for that."

Friendly applause from the dear colleagues thanking Zentis for the thanks. Which in turn allowed Zentis to applaud us, to thank us for having taken part in his exercise—or to thank us for the thanks for the thanks.

But the work had actually only just begun, he continued. These plans would have to be improved and optimized "for a day that hopefully will never come." But that was not the current task. We were only there to discuss and then adopt the preliminary report, which surely everybody had read. Nobody indicated otherwise, which meant, I was sure, that the preliminary report would become the final report. Zentis summarized it briefly. He didn't say a word about my "desertion," probably in exchange for my keeping my mouth shut. He surely didn't want to discuss the breakdown of all of Berlin's infrastructure resulting from his quarantine, which had been either outright stupid or come too late.

What was really remarkable, though, was that Zentis, always eager for applause and praise, didn't mention how much better "his" urban districts and "his" hospitals had handled the situation—despite the fact that Undersecretary Mueller was present. Had I overlooked something?

"We have put together a new folder for each of you for the work that now lies ahead of us. Mainly we are interested in your opinion on what would be different from our plague exercise if we were to be attacked in some other way. For instance, with other infectious agents, lethal gas, poison in our drinking water, dirty bombs, et cetera. Much of this comes from the Internet—there seems to be no shortage of ideas about how to kill us. We've even copied some blueprints on how a bacteriological or chemical bomb is constructed—but please don't try this at home!"

There was some friendly laughter at this remark, after which everybody happily took their folder, eager to make their escape this easily without a lengthy discussion on a report they'd never read.

"Any questions? If not, I think that's it for today."

Just then it dawned on me why Zentis hadn't bragged about his district's fantastic results. I realized that his total quarantine might not have been due to his overeagerness. I decided to test my theory.

"Just one question, Zentis. In certain urban areas and at certain hospitals, there were significantly lower rates of infection and death. Do you have an explanation for that?"

"That is correct. There are in fact some interesting differences in the way the fallout from the virtual terrorist attack was handled." He glanced in the direction of Undersecretary Mueller, who smiled back knowingly. "The reasons for this will have to be reviewed closely. We will probably have more on this at our next meeting."

What a fool I was! Of course Zentis hadn't let himself be celebrated there. By whom? His meager colleagues? That was of no interest to him—and perhaps even risky. In the end, his colleagues would read his report and see through his game. No, our sole function had been to approve his report. Undersecretary Mueller had obviously been made aware of Zentis's stellar results much earlier. Good old Zentis's aspirations went far beyond this undersecretary. He was waiting and preparing for a better occasion to flaunt his triumph.

It went against my nature to hold my tongue, but I decided to adopt Zentis's tactic. It was hard, but I could wait, too.

The meeting dissolved. As I was leaving, I turned around and saw Zentis looking at me with curiosity, perhaps even concern. I imagined he was wondering whether I presented a danger to his aspirations and, if so, what he should do about it.

CHAPTER 14

"I've never met your Dr. Zentis, but I know the type of windbag you're talking about. You usually find them in politics, as spokesmen for one thing or another."

That was a funny thing for Sommer to say. It seems that he'd forgotten that he himself was the spokesman for the Association of Small and Medium Enterprises. Perhaps it was because he was carefully shoveling a spoonful of lentils into his mouth while he was talking. Lentils were the undisputed culinary trend at all the plush restaurants around the Gendarmenmarkt this season. Sommer looked very content, I less so. I had lived on lentils for half my time in my med school—the other half of the time on spaghetti. Which was probably why I was complaining about Zentis.

"You know, Herr Sommer, you find this kind of person everywhere. As spokesman for some association in politics, but also in the medical field. I call it the A-student syndrome. These people have never really grown up and will do anything for a pat on the back, any kind of praise. Zentis is so eager to please! Last year he was the expert witness for the state attorney against a fellow cardiologist. This guy was notorious for putting stents into any coronary he could get ahold of, and he was finally sued for it. So expert witness Zentis said that yes, this guy was doing unnecessary interventions, which was true. He could have left it at that, but no, Zentis had to elaborate, describing his own expertise and exaggerating how many heart catheterizations he had performed himself. The attorney for the defendant made a quick calculation and realized that, going by these numbers, Mr. Expert Witness had performed more interventions every year than his defendant. Big laugh in court, case closed."

"Poor suckers, these people. Probably didn't get enough parental love and attention," Sommer speculated as he busied himself with a turnip gratin. Evidently turnips were the other hit of the season. Back to the roots!

"Sure, poor suckers, but also dangerous suckers. Not only because they always find enough people who believe and follow them—kindred spirits usually—but because they finally come to believe their own exaggerations. By the time this is over, Zentis will probably consider himself an expert on terrorist attacks from mail bombs to poison gas."

Sommer looked up from his turnips.

"This Zentis is also interested in poison gas?"

I shrugged. "I wouldn't be surprised."

"Listen, Dr. Hoffmann. If they go into poison gas and recruit you again, just remember that we're experts on all gases and how to transport and treat them."

Right. Sommer hadn't invited me on this excursion into the latest culinary trends to discuss Zentis's kindergarten psyche. He had business interests of course. He knew, for instance, that I was not only the interim department head of internal medicine, but also interim head of the clinical laboratory, and that surely it would have to be upgraded soon. But this wasn't about any specific business negotiation. Sommer was simply preserving a potentially valuable connection—in other words, buttering me up for some yet-to-be-determined reason. Had CEO Beate been with him, he would surely have bought all the roses that were being stuck under his nose at that very moment. He shook his head.

"I thought flower peddling in restaurants was in the hands of the Pakistanis!"

I watched as the flower peddler tried his luck at the next table. This one looked like he came from somewhere in the Middle East.

"No idea. Maybe with their seniority, the Pakistanis concentrate their efforts on the really lucrative places, not places like this, where people are dining out on their company's expense account. There just aren't enough young lovers here."

For dessert, Sommer indulged in a Cuban cigar, carefully selected from the restaurant's large humidor. I turned down the Havana but happily accepted the thirty-plus-year-old brandy whose name I hadn't even heard of. The cigar and brandy led to a few minutes of pleasant silence. Then Sommer sat up straight.

"Have you heard anything from your friend?"

"Heard from Celine?"

"Excuse me. I meant did they have any news for you at the embassy regarding what happened to her."

I told him about my visit there and the nice booklets about Iraq I had gotten out of it, but I didn't mention the latest rumor from Baran about Celine's shipment not having been clean. After all, Sommer had not only provided the trucks but also put up the money for the gas and the water purification plant. I would need more information before I could let him in on a possible "contamination" of the shipment. If the rumor were to prove true, Sommer should probably know nothing about it.

"I'll talk to the Iraqis about this myself, Dr. Hoffmann. I get along with them pretty well. And after all, we have to find out how to get the second half of your shipment there."

Celine's death and Heiner's disappearance weren't enough for him? Sommer noticed my surprise.

"But we have to know what really happened, don't we? And," he said, drinking the rest of his brandy, "as tragic as it was and as sorry as I am, these people are still in need of our help, don't you agree? Just think of all the equipment you people have already collected for a second shipment. It's just rotting away in the basement of your hospital, along with the second half of that mobile water purification system. It's not doing anyone any good there!"

For a capitalist, Sommer had an astonishingly soft heart.

CHAPTER 15

Granted, I take a certain pleasure in dinner invitations like Sommer's. Why should they commit me to anything? I get to enjoy the great cuisine and great wine and I just make sure I don't appear open to any kind of bribery. Which is quite simple: I just let myself be invited for excellent food and expensive wine by all the competitors.

"What do you think? Will Sommer make us a decent offer for upgrading the clinical lab?" Beate asked me at lunch the next day.

"We've still got time on that project. Let's first see how much dough we can swipe from the city. That should take care of a good chunk of it, especially for the microbiological lab, now that Zentis is making such a fuss about bioterrorism. Once we know how much money we need and where it will come from, we'll study the market and let the potential contractors invite us out to some more fancy dinners."

"Good idea. But let's not wait. Do it before these potential contractors find out that the real decision makers are sitting over at Vitalis headquarters and how little say an acting department head and CEO really have here. Go ahead and set some dates. I'm looking forward to it!"

Beate's cell phone played a little melody. She got up and nodded good-bye to me. Thus it remained unclear whether she was looking forward to the plush restaurants or to having dinner with charming Dr. Hoffmann. But she was right that ever more decisions were being moved from the individual hospitals to Vitalis headquarters. Keyword: synergistic effects. A fact I hoped to conceal for a while from our potential suppliers. But then, Herr Sommer was well aware of Vitalis's synergistic effects strategy. Why, then, had he still invited me for dinner, I wondered. Because of old times? Because I would be a full-fledged department head soon?

Walking back to my ward, I saw our Iraqi guest doctor coming my way. In reality, I just saw a cluster of nurses, nursing students, and female lab technicians. But it had become pretty safe to assume lately that when I saw a cluster of young—and even not-so-young—women at Berlin South, our guest doctor was at the center of it. As far as I could see, Dr. Hassan wasn't actively behind this. His good looks couldn't be held against him, nor could his exquisite politeness. I couldn't help but wonder, however, if he interacted with women with the same civility in his home country. Seeing me, he broke away from his escort and took me aside.

"I spoke to my brother-in-law in Baghdad at some length yesterday. He's asked around but he has learned nothing about the fate of your friend yet."

"There's been nothing in the papers about a bomb attack?"

"Not a word, but that doesn't mean a thing. In Iraq the government decides what you can read in the paper. If a bomb attack doesn't fit in with the current propaganda, it has not taken place."

"And the street? Nothing through the grapevine?"

"Nothing that my brother-in-law has heard."

"But isn't it strange that your government would inform my government about a bomb attack and not have the papers report on it?"

Dr. Hassan shrugged.

"In Iraq? Not really."

Did my—or rather Celine's—Kurdish friends, with their rumor that her shipment wasn't clean, have better connections in Iraq than Dr. Hassan? Or did the Kurds just adhere more closely to the tradition of 1,001 nights of storytelling? If nothing else, it was clear that they and Hassan's brother-in-law relied on different sources, a fact that might come in handy someday if some piece of information from there ever needed to be confirmed.

"Excuse me. What did you say?"

Dr. Hassan had gone on talking while I was thinking and had just asked me something.

"I was just wondering what was going to happen now with all that medication and material?"

He was referring to the second shipment, which was rotting away in the basement of the old building.

"I have no idea. For the moment, at least."

"I can understand that, Herr Hoffmann. Would you mind if I gave some thought to how to get the shipment to its destination?"

Why should I mind? As Herr Sommer had reminded me only the previous day, that stuff wasn't doing anyone any good down in the basement.

Ever since the Foreign Office had informed me of Celine's death, I hadn't given much thought to what should happen to the equipment in the basement or how to get it to Kurdistan, other than giving a key to the basement to Baran. It would certainly have stayed that way if two people hadn't reminded me of it independently of each other and if Marianne hadn't given birth to her first child when she did. Marianne was married to Martin, who was a first-year resident in my department. Martin was scheduled for a night shift when his wife went into labor.

"What can I do, Herr Hoffmann? They seem to be real contractions. She isn't due until next week!"

On any normal day, Martin was a competent and prudent young doctor. But not that day. Otherwise, he would have known to trust our duty roster rather than what the obstetricians had calculated. Because everybody knows that your first child always comes when you're scheduled for night duty or headed out of town to present a paper at some scientific conference. Furthermore, he would have remembered that there was a column in the duty roster indicating who his replacement would be. Although, even if he had remembered, he probably would have had trouble dialing his replacement's telephone number correctly.

"Just get out of here, Martin. I'll call your backup to take care of your night duty. And all the best to your wife!"

His wife would have to make it without my best wishes, because by then Martin was long gone.

I checked the time. It was a little after seven p.m. I uploaded the duty roster on the internal IT system and tried to get Marion, Martin's benchwarmer, on the phone. No luck, just her voice mail. Cell phone: same luck. Rather than call my other colleagues and listen to multiple variations of why it was a bad night for them to fill in, I decided that I could wait for Marion to call back and work on the latest stuff to pile up on my desk. I started with the easy task of reading and signing off on my residents' patient reports to their respective GP colleagues.

By the time Marion called back ("Sorry, I was in the shower, blah blah blah…"), I told her not to come and to just continue her body restoration. I would just stay at the hospital and continue tackling my paperwork. Which meant that I wouldn't have to drag the load home, where nobody was waiting for me anyway, nor in the apartment across the street.

It turned out to be a rather quiet night for a change, which meant that by midnight all the paperwork was done. I didn't feel like going to bed yet and decided it might be a good idea to check on our second shipment in the basement. Some of the medication was probably getting close to its expiration date and would have to be exchanged at our hospital pharmacy.

I found the door to the basement in the old building unlocked and ajar. When was the last time I'd been down there? Probably with Celine. Could we have left the door open? Or had Baran been down there since Celine's funeral, when I'd given him the second key? Whatever, no big deal. Judging by the standards of a prosperous first-world country, there was nothing much worth stealing, and no illegal drugs.

I checked the antibiotics and noted down which had to be replaced. After that, I made sure that the airtight packaging of the medical equipment, like the cast-off respirators or infusion pumps, hadn't become prey to hungry rats. Granted, envisioning rats in a hospital basement was not a very pleasant notion, but why should our signs—"Please no potted plants or animals inside the hospital"—scare away these intelligent rodents? It seemed more conceivable that, given our abundant use of chemicals and radioactivity, we might have bred some especially ravenous mutants.

But it had definitely not been rats who had opened the big wooden crate in the back, which contained the second half of Sommer's water purification plant. A hammer and a crowbar were still lying next to it. Suddenly I heard a noise. Again, definitely not rats.

"Anybody there?"

Without question, the single dumbest possible question I could have asked! I reached for the crowbar. Which seemed better than trying to remember the tricks Celine had shown me from her self-defense training.

Now I heard a cautious scratching or scuffling. "Anybody there" was clearly on the move. To try to escape or to better position himself to attack? I lifted the crowbar above my head and took a step forward, in the direction of the door. At least I knew where I wanted to go.

Beep—beep—beep. "Dr. Hoffmann. Urgent. Nurse Station 3B. Urgent. Nurse Station 3B," the display on my pager read, giving me a legitimate reason to beat a hasty retreat. Which I was more than happy to do. After all, who can be absolutely certain that mutated monster-rats only exist in Hollywood B movies?

Twenty minutes later, I returned to the basement. Enough time for whoever it was to get lost. Which I checked thoroughly. The case I'd been paged about hadn't really been urgent, of course. By the time I got there, the patient had even forgotten why he'd wanted to see a doctor. A memory lapse that might have had something to do with seeing, in the dim nighttime illumination, a doctor standing at his bedside with a crowbar in his hand.

I put the crowbar aside and had a look at the broken-up crate. Is that what a mobile water purification plant looked like? Or, rather, half of it? I had no idea. I found it more irritating that the piece of equipment I was staring at rang some bell in my mind.

The rest of the night was rather uneventful. Around three in the morning, my patient Herr Schlups, who was to finally get his cardiac pacemaker implanted in the morning, urgently wanted to see me. He had signed the informed consent form two days before but had only just read it. I assured him that despite all the threats listed on this form, I would not perforate his heart muscle nor let him bleed to death.

I spent the remaining hours until the official start of the hospital day on the narrow couch in my office, trying to remember everyone who had a key to the old building's basement door. Probably a lot more people than I was aware of. After that, I stayed awake pondering why that purification plant machine looked so familiar. Finally, our cafeteria opened for breakfast.

Right after breakfast, I was ready to put that pacemaker into Herr Schlups. As he was being rolled into the operating room, he greeted me with confidence. After all, the informed consent form didn't mention the risk that you might be operated on by a tired doctor after his night shift.

CHAPTER 16

Implanting a pacemaker is routine business, at least for a clinical cardiologist. It is performed with only local anesthesia and takes somewhere between fifteen and thirty minutes. So after making some introductory remarks and finding a suitable vein, I tried to make some sense of my adventures in the basement the night before as I tested the best location for the cables in Herr Schlups's heart. Who had been sneaking around down there and busying himself with that crate? Tracking all people who possibly had a key to the basement wouldn't get me anywhere, nor would trying to recall everyone who knew about the equipment down there in the first place. That was a significant number of people, most of whom could have been there without needing to hide from me. Like Baran from Kurdistan, for example, or our guest doctor, Abdul Hassan. Even Herr Sommer could have been there on official business, to check on his machine.

Meanwhile, I was satisfied with the location of the cables, mechanically and electrically, and only had to bury the little box with the battery and the electronics. This is not especially challenging, either intellectually or technically, so I continued with my line of thinking. However, no prime suspect came to my mind. I tried taking a scientific approach, whereby you look at things from another perspective when your hypothesis runs into a dead end. I would start by thinking not about who the prime suspect might be but about the broken crate, or rather its contents, and ask myself who could be interested in half a mobile water purification plant, and why. The age-old question arose: Who would profit?

As I reflected on this matter, a few thousand euros' worth of medical technology had vanished into Herr Schlups. I just had to make a few stitches to close the wound.

"All done."

"And—all went well, Herr Doctor?"

"A-OK!" I assured Herr Schlups.

A small tear appeared in his left eye.

"Thank you, Doctor. I could see how much you were concentrating on your work. You didn't say a word!"

Indeed! I usually chatted with the assisting nurse and the patient on a routine job like this. But this time, with my fingers on autopilot, I had been so wrapped up in my own thoughts that the whole procedure had been like a silent film.

"You're welcome, Herr Schlups!"

I had the rest of the day all planned: After my vigil, my residents would have to do patient rounds on their own and save up their questions for me for the following day. I planned to go home early, have a little nap, and then get to work on that new perspective on what had happened in the basement. I was just embarking on the first part of my plan—breaking the new schedule to the residents—when my cell phone rang. It was Beate.

"Felix, I have a journalist on the other line. He wants information on how well prepared we are in case of a terrorist attack, whether we could handle the plague or anthrax, stuff like that. Can you take over?"

The call didn't come as a surprise.

"Sure. Put him through."

Of course this wasn't just a coincidence. This journalist, evidently one who still bothered talking to people rather than just cobbling together his information from Google, had been invited to a press conference about bioterrorism at the Berlin Department of Internal Affairs. It finally became clear where Zentis planned to spread the news of how well he had handled the plague-situation in "his" hospitals and urban districts.

"When is this press conference going to happen?"

"Tomorrow morning."

I quickly reached an agreement with the journalist: I would not only feed him some background information, but I'd also give him some good questions to ask. In return, he would take me along.

"Do we have a deal?"

"We do, Dr. Hoffmann. See you tomorrow."

I liked the deal. But it meant I would be at this press conference the next morning and not at Berlin South. So I couldn't put off making the rounds with my residents after all and I gave up going home early to have a nice nap. Brooding over the new perspective would also have to wait. But then, what don't you do to surprise an old friend!

CHAPTER 17

This time, local officials had splurged on canapés and orange juice. Anything to please the press! I was hungry and would have liked to help myself to a few hors d'oeuvres, but I decided to hang back. Given that our city's secretary of the interior was to honor us by making the news public himself, I gathered that only good news was to be presented. Next to him was Comrade Zentis. Undersecretary Mueller was relegated to the second row. Seated directly behind his boss, he was just a stooge at this press conference.

Zentis gave a short overview of the exercise and described how "resolutely, efficiently, and seriously" it had been handled, thanks to the "outstanding medical and organizational competence" of the team. At this, he looked bashfully at the ground. The secretary of the interior stressed how lucky we were to have a city government that made provisions for catastrophes like the one in this exercise. Then the floor was opened to questions.

As I'd expected, I had not been the only one feeding questions to the press. Some journalist was already pointing to the graphs showing how different parts of the city had performed and wanted to know why Marzahn and Hellersdorf had done so much better, with, specifically, almost 50 percent fewer casualties than the rest of Berlin. The secretary of the interior handed the question over to Dr. Zentis, "who was responsible for planning, organizing, and coordinating the entire exercise."

Dr. Zentis was more than happy to answer.

"Allow me to begin by pointing out that everyone on this team gave his best, as did all the hospitals that took part in the exercise. But in a big city like Berlin, you will naturally always find differences." All he could say to explain the difference was that it looked like the patients in Marzahn and Hellersdorf had gotten somewhat superior medical treatment.

At this, my journalist wanted to jump in, but I held him back. I was sure that Zentis had ordered at least one more question. Which he had indeed.

"Weren't you personally responsible for the work in the hospitals for those two districts, in addition to coordinating the entire exercise?"

Zentis looked taken aback by this question, as though he found it a bit embarrassing, but—casting his eyes down again—he had to admit that, yes, he had been responsible.

I didn't need to tell my man that this was his cue.

"Dr. Zentis, since you were personally responsible for these hospitals, first allow me to congratulate you. Please don't be offended by my question: Could this be a simple coincidence?"

Zentis swallowed the bait.

"I'm not offended, not at all. But no, it's not a coincidence. We had significantly fewer casualties in every one of the three hospitals compared to every other hospital in Berlin."

"Do you have an explanation for the different results?"

Zentis said that the data were still being analyzed, and looked as though he wanted to move on to another question. Alas, my friend didn't yet.

"Of course I'm just a layman. But could it be that certain hospitals in your exercise had a larger quantity of certain antibiotics on hand than others?"

Zentis smiled. "The amount of medication on hand is each hospital's own responsibility. There is no law regarding the quantity or sort of medication that a facility has to keep in stock. Any more questions?"

"What I wanted to know, and please excuse my insistence," my journalist went on, "is whether the hospitals you were responsible for were able to hand out more antibiotics, even for primary prevention? In other words, had they been better prepared for this exercise than the other hospitals?"

It was a blink of an eye, nothing more. As the only one who had awaited the question, I was probably the only one who noticed this fleeting hesitation from Zentis. But I was definitely not the only one who saw Herr Secretary give him a questioning look.

"Thank you for this important question. Perhaps I haven't made this clear enough. It was an integral part of our exercise to compare hospitals that had received advance warning to those that had not." Zentis turned to Herr Secretary. "This way, we were able to show how important it is to make provisions for such attacks. That is this study's message to the decision makers in politics."

I was pretty sure that Zentis hadn't expected anybody to find out, least of all some journalist. The walls were plastered with graphs and statistics. I had to congratulate him on his lightning-quick reaction. If I hadn't known him for years, he would have convinced me, too.

"Yes?" With a wry smile, he had to give the floor to my journalist once more.

"One more question, regarding the timing of the quarantine you imposed on the city. Among other consequences, it resulted in other hospitals not being able to stock up on the antibiotics they needed, which further favored 'your' hospitals. Would you care to comment?"

Zentis's eyes moved away from the journalist and scanned the room. When his gaze finally landed on me, his face went white. His answer, given through clenched teeth, was hardly audible. I understood only one thing for sure: I had a friend for life.

Bundesamt für Verfassungsschutz
Dept. III, File #0423-54
Anonymous telephone call
Original recording
Caller: male voice, as yet unidentified

Operator: "Your call has been forwarded to me because you said you had information on a possible terrorist attack. Please begin by giving me your name."

Caller: "I have a name for you. Dr. Hoffmann. Dr. Felix Hoffmann."

Operator: "And your address, Dr. Hoffmann?"

Caller: "I am not Dr. Hoffmann. But Dr. Hoffmann is somebody who should be of interest to you. You will find his address in the phone book."

Operator: "And why should this Dr. Hoffmann be of interest to us?"

Caller: "You would find out if you were to search his home and find the kind of documents he is storing there."

Operator: "This is quite vague and not enough for us to act on. We would need more specific information in order to proceed with a search."

Caller: "I find it my citizen's duty to inform the proper authorities when somebody is collecting blueprints for biological and chemical bombs. I have seen such blueprints at Hoffmann's home myself."

Operator: "Yes, that would indeed be most interesting. Wouldn't you like to give us your name in case we have any queries?"

Caller hung up. Call originated from a pay phone at Zoo train station.

Assessment: Said Dr. Felix Hoffmann already listed as a Suspect Category C, which gives the call, although anonymous, some credibility.

Suggested action: Upgrading Dr. Felix Hoffmann to Suspect Category B. Further action worth considering.

Bundesamt für Verfassungsschutz
Memo
Ref: Felix Hoffmann, MD
Status: Suspect Category B

Court declined search warrant due to "insufficient grounds."
Interception of telephone communications was also denied.
Suggested action: Special operations
[Signature illegible]

CHAPTER 18

Friday night I worked overtime to make up for the time I spent at the press conference. But, more important, my friend Michael Thiel had promised to come by. Michael had once been one of the senior doctors in our hospital's lab before starting his own private medical laboratory with attractive female technicians and excellent machinery. I wanted to see him because of his excellent machinery—or, more precisely, his technical expertise—because I wanted him to have a look at that thing in the broken-up crate.

We headed down into the basement, where I waited eagerly while Michael thoroughly inspected the apparatus.

"This is no water purification plant. Never in a million years!"

I had suspected as much by that point, but still I asked.

"You sure?"

"Absolutely! I have no idea what it is. But just have a look at these gaskets. And these valves. They're not for your normal water tube or ordinary water pump. These gaskets are extremely resilient and secure, which means they're not for liquids, but for gases. For gases under high pressure that shouldn't leak under any circumstances. Never in your life would you use these superexpensive gaskets and valves for a mere water purification plant, mobile or not."

I sat down on the hard concrete floor. Things were slowly starting to make some sense. Celine had been used, Heiner had been used, I had been used. Michael, of course, also saw that.

"You guys have been useful idiots. Your good friend Herr Sommer integrates these high-tech gaskets and valves into a water purification plant—if that's even what this is—and that's how he bypasses the embargo and Saddam Hussein gets the strategic parts his engineers and generals need so badly."

Michael was probably right. German industry, especially mid-sized enterprises, had a proud tradition of helping out embargo-impaired dictators around the world. I recalled how Imhausen Chemicals had provided General Gadhafi with a complete factory for poison gas—turnkey ready—back in the eighties. Suddenly it came to me why that thing in the wooden crate looked familiar. I got up, dusting my pants off.

"Let's go have a beer at my place, Michael. There's something I'd like to show you."

Back at my place, Michael had to wait while I tried to find what I was looking for: the pictures of and blueprints for biobombs, gas grenades, and so on that Zentis had worked into his dossier. Too many beers? Too many night shifts? Too many years? I was pretty sure I'd put the folders in interim storage on the ever-growing to-be-taken-care-of-later stack on my bookshelf. But no, they weren't to be found there. Had I studied them in bed? At my desk? At the kitchen table? They weren't there, either. I finally tracked them down on the bookshelf, but in the wrong stack, the will-take-care-of-itself-alone one. Strange. I couldn't imagine that I'd ever thought that Zentis's games would take care of themselves on their own.

"Something wrong?" Michael asked over his beer.

I ignored his question, because I knew I could show him what kind of humanitarian help we had stored in my hospital's basement: a high-performance, heavy-duty atomizer, crucial for the large-scale production of poison gas. Germany, land of fine scientific and engineering traditions!

"Shit! You're right, Felix. This looks almost exactly like that thing you have down there."

Which meant that we weren't storing half of something in the basement, but the real complete thing. Or, inversely, that Celine and Heiner had already transported at least one of these atomizers to Iraq.

Michael helped himself to another beer.

"So what do we do now?"

I was most grateful for his "we," but I didn't have the answer. Michael, however, came up with a practical proposal.

"We should get that thing out of there until we know what to do with it. Otherwise, it might get into the wrong hands," he said, reaching for his cell phone.

I was happy that somebody had taken the initiative.

"We can get a truck on Sunday. For free," Michael said.

"Great. But where do we take that thing?"

"We drive it to my grandmother's farm, a good fifty miles from here. I already have all kinds of stuff left over from my divorce stored in her barn. She won't mind. Perhaps she can put it to some use, making cider or something."

It seemed like a good first step. But it didn't go according to plan. When Michael pulled up in front of Berlin South on Sunday morning with the truck and a bright grin on his face, we found the door to the basement neatly locked for a change. But the alleged water purification plant had vanished. Did somebody else need it for cider production?

CHAPTER 19

Beate had enjoyed the weekend in the vicinity of Berlin, attending what certainly must have been a most thrilling conference with all the CEOs in the Vitalis holding. Which is why I hadn't called her about my latest discovery. We had tentative plans to meet for dinner that night, so that she could fill me in on the latest news from headquarters. So I called her on the phone.

"Felix, I'm done for this weekend, but I'm dead tired and hitting the sack early."

"Sorry, Beate, but your bed will have to wait a little longer for you." Without going into detail, I told her we had to meet right then and that I was on my way. "Make yourself a cup of strong coffee. I'll pick up Chinese food. We'll need some time."

Half an hour later, Beate opened her door for me in her bathrobe. It was the first time I'd ever seen her without makeup. Did that indicate a higher degree of intimacy between us? Or that she simply didn't care what I thought of her?

She hadn't made coffee. Instead, she opened a bottle of wine while I told her about the apparatus in the hospital's basement.

"Could it be some kind of sick joke? Or that both of you are wrong?"

"Sorry, no sick joke. And no, we're not wrong." I showed her the pictures and blueprints from Zentis's folder. "See here. That's exactly what it is."

Beate studied the documents thoroughly, reviewing the details on performance, production capacity, and suggested applications.

"Oh God, this is appalling! We have to get rid of this machine at once. Or, better yet, hand it over to the police. The sooner, the better, Felix!"

"Too late."

I told her why.

"All the more reason to call the police. Or the BND. Or the Verfassungsschutz. I have no idea whose jurisdiction it is."

Probably unconsciously, Beate helped herself to a second glass of wine. I had done most of the talking and only then took my first sip.

"I suggest we wait a little while before we spread the news. At least until we've found out what this has to do with Celine."

Beate put her glass down on the table much too firmly.

"We know what this has to do with Celine. It killed her!"

Unlike Beate, I'd had all day to mull that over.

"That's precisely what doesn't add up. OK, our Iraqi friends want to produce poison gas and desperately need this piece of equipment. Celine brings them one, along with her humanitarian aid. But she was unaware of it, so why should they kill her?"

A strand of hair kept falling into Beate's face, which she kept putting back behind her ear. Finally, she gave up and rolled it around her finger.

"Well, Celine might have seen the thing. For example, when it was unloaded."

"Again, it doesn't add up. Number one: Celine went to the Kurdish part of Iraq. I'm pretty sure the Iraqis don't dare to show up there. Number two: the thing was packed in a wooden crate. Number three: let's suppose that crate fell off the truck while they were unloading it and the machine was plainly visible. Or that the Iraqis had the nerve to track down Celine and even opened the crate while she was watching. She'd simply have seen some machine and thought, just as we did, that it was part of that water plant."

"What about her friend Heiner in the second truck?"

"What about him? Heiner is—or was—a botanist. How would he have recognized it as an atomizer?"

At least that was what Celine had told me when she'd introduced Heiner to me. Which probably only meant that was what Heiner had told her. So was he really a botanist? Or, in fact, an engineer working for Herr Sommer? No, that was paranoid. Or was it? How long had Celine known this Heiner before her Iraq mission?

And if Celine had somehow found out what had been slipped to her, how would she have reacted? I found it conceivable that this might have turned my pacifist friend into a very angry person. Perhaps even into a person who would throw a bomb? I told Beate my latest thoughts.

"You really find that conceivable, Felix?"

"Not really."

But I wasn't *entirely* sure. And I was distracted. While we'd been talking, Beate's bathrobe had slipped opened a bit, revealing glimpses of her thighs and a hazy notion of more. Good God! Had I never seen thighs before? We were talking about Celine here! What was wrong with me? Was it just a reflex running straight to the spinal cord and back without ever getting near the brain? Or was I a monster, emotionally at least, unable to mourn Celine but always ready for a sexual adventure? I did have one thing on my side at least, but one glass of wine wasn't much of an excuse.

"Is something wrong, Felix?"

Was the fact that Beate was tightening her bathrobe a subconscious gesture? In any case, I was able to get back on track.

"Perhaps Celine's pacifism didn't survive the test of reality."

"Well, it survived the test here in Germany," Beate countered.

Had CEO Beate turned into a revolutionary? Was she really comparing Saddam Hussein's Iraq to Germany, a model student of democracy for the last sixty years? But uncertain about Celine's possible actions and motivation—and even more uncertain about my own possible actions and motivation—I let Beate's remark go without comment and wished her a good night. Which got me a kiss from her. I closed my eyes, because the bathrobe had begun to present its low neckline to me.

"Be careful, Felix. Not everybody will believe that you had nothing to do with the disappearance of that ultra-whatever-it-is atomizer and that you don't know its whereabouts."

Whoa! That had never occurred to me.

CHAPTER 20

By the following Tuesday, at the very latest, I would have hit upon that idea on my own. When I had finished rounds, I found Herr Sommer sitting in my office. He must have let himself in. He was there, he explained, because he had promised me at our recent dinner to look into ways to get the second aid shipment to Kurdistan.

"But, Dr. Hoffmann, it seems that part of the shipment is missing. Are you storing parts of it at a different location?"

For a moment I was puzzled. How would Sommer know where we had stored the stuff? But then I realized that he would simply have asked Mr. Sobotka, his on-site construction manager. Sommer had asked Sobotka to help us load the trucks for Celine's trip, which he had done—albeit reluctantly. Could it have been Sommer that I had heard creeping around in the basement the other night? A German industrialist tiptoeing around behind dusty crates of medication and equipment destined for Kurdistan? It was hard to imagine. All the more so because Sommer, knowing its contents, wouldn't have had to break it open. I looked at him quizzically.

"When did you go down to in the basement?"

"Just now. While you were doing your rounds. I can't waste my time waiting around."

The man's arrogance was irritating. Although I couldn't see the precise connection between his little extra shipment and Celine's death, I held him responsible for it—or most of it.

"You have absolutely no right to go roaming around the basement of Berlin South as though this was your company, Herr Sommer. Without our permission, you have no business there, or, for that matter, in my office."

Sommer remained undeterred.

"Where is my water purification plant, Dr. Hoffmann?"

"*Your* water purification plant? Everything in this basement belongs to the people it has been donated to."

I felt pretty proud of that sentence. It could have come directly from Celine. Then again, I found it sounded a little goofy.

"That's ridiculous, Dr. Hoffmann! Have you been sleeping with *The Communist Manifesto* under your pillow lately? I have neither donated this equipment to some legitimate aid organization, nor has it ever officially come under your ownership. As long as it's sitting here in Berlin, it's all mine." He drew his face closer. "So just tell me where you dragged my damn water plant."

I was sure that Sommer knew the real function of his alleged water purification plant, but decided to play dumb for the time being. All the more so because, even if I had wanted to, I couldn't tell him where the hell it was.

"Herr Sommer! We are all deeply indebted to you for the help you have given on our project. But I think that from here on out, we'd rather continue our work without your involvement."

I often spoke in that stilted way when I was annoyed. It drives people nuts! Sommer was no exception. He jumped to his feet, red-faced with anger.

"I'll tell you something, Hoffmann: you will never become department head in this hospital. That I can guarantee you! And one more thing I can guarantee you: you will tell me where you're hiding my machinery before long."

Being the well-brought-up person I am, I also stood. I opened the door for him. After all, he had been my guest.

CHAPTER 21

I was sure Herr Sommer would keep his promise that I would never become department head. But my chances hadn't been too great in the first place. As for Sommer, he had demonstrated his strong connections with Vitalis's management just the other day at the official ceremony for his newly installed systems in our surgery department. Yet something else became clear to me only then: he hadn't invited me to dinner at the Gendarmenmarkt in hopes of laying the groundwork for any future contract. He was well aware how little say acting department head Dr. Hoffmann had in such important matters and had probably stitched up any deal he wanted at the proper level long ago. Our dinner had been all about the second shipment to Iraq. His friends there were probably badgering him day and night about when they would finally be able to get their poison-gas production up and running. I was sure they only planned to pay up after it had been delivered.

At the moment, though, I had no time for Herr Sommer's problems. Dr. Hassan had asked me urgently to stop by to discuss our patient Mr. Krauskopf. We had lost the battle over his right kidney, and the surgeons had removed it after all. We were still hoping that his left kidney would compensate for the loss eventually, but for the time being Mr. Krauskopf was still hooked up to a kidney machine.

"I wouldn't put my money on it," our guest doctor said. "These aminoglycoside antibiotics can be pretty nephrotoxic, and in this case, they were. They didn't clear up the infection in the right kidney, nor did they do his left one any good. Chances are, we've lost that one, too."

"Too early to say. Perhaps we'll get lucky. Or, rather, Herr Krauskopf will."

We then took a look at the other patients on dialysis. Among them was our cost-intensive Herr Cornelsen, whom we still hadn't gotten rid of. By and large, Dr. Hassan was doing a good job and had become a real help in the nephrology department.

"Have you got time for a coffee, Herr Hoffmann?"

"Sure. Let's have it in your office."

Office was a somewhat exaggerated term for the broom closet Hassan shared with two other doctors from nephrology, but it gave us enough privacy for the moment.

"Remember how I promised to give your second shipment to Iraq some thought?"

"Yes, you said as much."

"That's why I went to have a look at your stock in the basement."

Which led to the same question I had just asked Herr Sommer.

"When did you do that?"

"Yesterday afternoon."

If that was true, it hadn't been our guest doctor that I had disturbed the other night. Still, it was remarkable how many people were suddenly eager to get our shipment on its way!

"And, once more," Dr. Hassan continued, "last night, when I showed your stock to my cousin. His brother-in-law runs a trucking company that goes to Iran twice or even three times a month.

That would mean reloading it only once, somewhere in Turkey probably."

"And this brother in law would take our stuff for free?"

"Probably not the whole load at once, but yes, one or two pieces per trip, depending on the space he has left."

Could I trust this offer? Hassan's next question made me wonder about that.

"Is that the entire shipment in the basement? Didn't you mention some mobile water purification plant?"

Had I mentioned the plant to Hassan? It would have helped me enormously at that moment if I could remember. But I had no time to brood about it, as we were called back to Mr. Krauskopf just then, who was experiencing trouble with his blood pressure on the kidney machine. Once that was taken care of, there was something else Hassan wanted to tell me.

"One more thing, Herr Hoffmann. Not the best of news though, I'm afraid. My brother-in-law has heard rumors that a foreign woman threw a bomb inside or at the gate of a military base."

Oh God! Until the Sunday before, when for the first time I had accepted the possibility, however small, of Celine having exploded a bomb, I would have been sure that Hassan had been fed this news directly by Saddam's secret police, or, that he was, in fact, part of that police. Not anymore. And yet, how convenient for all interested parties that I got this confirmation from an unofficial source. Could I trust anybody? And if so, who?

I don't recall how I replied to Hassan or whether I even said anything at all. I do remember, however, that I stormed directly into Beate's office.

"Have you got the files on this Dr. Hassan?"

"Did something happen, Felix?"

I gave her a short version of our conversation.

"So, in light of all that," I said, "don't you find it suspicious that we all of a sudden get this hot deal? A competent, fluent German-speaking doctor from Iraq for free?"

Under normal circumstances, Beate would have teased me that I was just envious of Dr. Hassan and his popularity with the female staff. Instead, though, she just handed me his file. I quickly found what I was looking for.

"Born in Samarra, Iraq. Any idea where that is?"

Beate didn't know. That night, at home, I found the city on the big map on which Celine had sketched her route.

Samarra was about forty miles south of Tikrit, where I knew that Saddam Hussein recruited his most reliable personnel. It was his birthplace and the ancestral seat of his clan. Forty miles from that madman's home turf was far too close for my taste.

Bundesamt für Verfassungsschutz
Dept. IV, File #286-56
Subject: Felix Hoffmann, MD

Based on an anonymous telephone call, Dept. III ordered special operations. Detailed information and blueprints on the production of explosives as well as bacteriological and chemical grenades were found in the apartment of the subject (see numeric listing in appendix).

Interviews with neighbors produced no tangible leads. All neighbors agreed, however, that the subject demonstrates no repetitive daily routine, but rather a suspicious lifestyle in which he repeatedly disappears for entire nights.

All persons interviewed were sworn to secrecy.

Assessment: The above findings suggest with a probability verging on certainty that suspect Hoffmann is actively preparing for terrorist attacks, probably on German territory. Considering the suspect's known connections to Kurdish expatriates (see photo-documentation from suspect Celine Bergkamp), attacks on Iraqi institutions in Germany must be considered a possibility.

Suggested further action: Surveillance of subject is to be continued.

Material found so far does not indicate that the subject is considering immediate action.

Cross-references: suspect Celine Ulrike Bergkamp, suspect Heiner Schmidt, United Democrats of Kurdistan.

Appendix: Information and blueprints pertaining to the production of explosives, as well as bacteriological and chemical grenades, found in the apartment of suspect Hoffmann (for tactical reasons, the original material was photographed as future evidence but left in situ).
[Signature illegible]
Handwritten side note: Iraqi embassy located in immediate vicinity of suspect's place of residence!!

CHAPTER 22

The following evening I had unexpected company. My guests were waiting for me at my door after I climbed the stairs, annoyed that I'd once again had to park two blocks away. As had been the case several times lately, my usual parking space was blocked by some light truck from a plumbing service. Had one of my female neighbors developed a taste for tough handymen? Probably, because the truck often stayed overnight.

My visitor, however, was not some tough handyman. The two gentlemen at my door were wearing dark suits. In their midtwenties, I guessed, one was black, the other looked Irish, with red hair with freckles. Were they American Mormons trying to save my soul?

It was their shoes that gave them away. They were too shiny even for Mormons. These shoes not only reflected the light from the lamps on the ceiling, but I could probably have even used them as a mirror when shaving. Which undoubtedly meant American military or something close to it. The Irish guy put it a little differently.

"We're here on behalf of the US government."

Unlike Jablonske and Waldeck from our native Verfassungsschutz, that was all the proof they seemed to feel was necessary. They showed no ID, no badge.

"Do you have any proof?"

"You're welcome to call our embassy."

"And ask for the cultural attaché, right?"

I waived the call to their embassy and let the gentlemen in. They introduced themselves as Mr. McGilly and Mr. Thorne. It seemed there was even an American dimension to this mess! Interesting, to say the least. Because I was rather sure that this visit was about Iraq and/or Kurdistan. I could think of no other reason why the US government wanted to talk to Dr. Hoffmann.

And I was right. For the most part, they asked the same questions as Jablonske and Waldeck had the other night. Unlike their German colleagues, however, they were not much interested in Celine. They grew more curious as soon I mentioned Herr Sommer. How long had I known him? Did I know anything about his private life? Had I ever been to his factory? To his home? Did I know any of his friends?

"And how did it come about that Mr. Sommer offered his company's trucks for your friend's relief transport?"

"We blackmailed him."

"Blackmailed?"

So far, our conversation had been in German. It was not clear if they didn't know the German word for *blackmail* or just didn't believe me. So I repeated in English that we had blackmailed Herr Sommer.

"At the time," I continued in English, "I had some say in the hospital regarding who would get the contract for installing new gas tubes in our operating theaters. When I talked to Sommer about it, I hinted that helping with that transport might make my decision easier. Honestly, though, it wasn't really blackmail. It seems that we would have gotten his trucks either way, as he was genuinely interested in my friend's project."

The US government representatives nodded in agreement. Both evidently thought as much. Redhead got down to the crux of the matter.

"Was that all you got from Herr Sommer, the two trucks?"

Of course, I knew where this was going, but why make it too easy for them?

"No, that wasn't all. He also gave us money for some diesel."

I knew that *diesel* was street slang for heroin in English, so it was a mean word to throw in.

"Diesel, huh?"

Thorne jumped in.

"What we really want to know is whether Sommer donated some technical equipment from his company for the Kurds."

It occurred to me that this was a detail Jablonske and Waldeck hadn't followed up on, even after I'd mentioned it to them.

"Yes, right. A mobile water purification plant from his factory."

Again I saw no reason to let the pair in on my latest findings.

"And, where is it now, this water purification plant?"

"Half of it should be in Kurdistan. That was the plan, at least."

Thorne, the African-American, leaned significantly closer to me.

"And the other half, Dr. Hoffmann?"

"Lost in follow-up."

That was a term we used for medical statistics, but the two got my meaning. Both said that they were very sorry about the disappearance—and then offered a somewhat surprising explanation for their disappointment.

"You should consider our technical and logistical resources for the shipment of such equipment, Dr. Hoffmann. You're sure you really don't know where it is?"

"I'm sorry, but no."

They had a few more questions, but they were clearly dissatisfied with me. I had the impression that they were no longer paying much attention to my answers, that something else preoccupied them. Perhaps the question of who they should ask for permission to actively jog my memory regarding the whereabouts of Sommer's gift. Their cultural attaché, most probably.

German national television, Channel 1 News

A Pentagon spokesman disclosed today that a joint
US-British air attack took place on an Iraqi military installation south of the thirty-sixth parallel. During a routine patrol within the no-fly
zone north of the thirty-sixth parallel, an Iraqi
air-defense radar locked in on the fighters, the
Pentagon said. The Iraqi military installation has
been largely destroyed, with no allied casualties.

CHAPTER 23

After my guests left, I helped myself to a beer and thought, To hell with McGilly and Thorne. It was clear that they and the US government were only interested in Sommer's alleged water purification plant, and couldn't care less about what had happened to Celine. Which was why, as they would have put it, I had "withheld information" and hadn't elaborated on what I'd learned about that water plant. The day might come when I could put this limited knowledge to better use than sharing it with a couple of US agents. That said, I still didn't know who had hidden the damn thing or where.

I wondered how I should spend the rest of my evening. I didn't feel like reading or dictating patient reports, and the TV networks, I discovered, didn't feel like airing anything worth my time. But it was too early for bed, and I was too wound up by my house call from the American government. Thank God for the Internet—with e-mails and chat rooms and any number of nuts online—to pass the time.

While my laptop took its sweet time warming up, I made a mental list of all the people who had asked me about the whereabouts of that vanished water plant. Herr Sommer, our noble benefactor. Guest doctor Abdul Hassan (and, through him, the Iraqi secret police?). And the United States of America. Could I assume that each of these parties had asked out of genuine interest and was not simply trying to cover its tracks? That none of them had swiped it from the basement themselves? If that was the case, the question remained: Who did?

I went on making my list. Our brave Verfassungsschutz? My friend Michael? Both struck me as improbable. Like I said, Jablonske and Waldeck had shown no interest in the plant, even after I'd mentioned it to them. And I didn't think Michael suddenly wanted to go into the poison-gas business, or that he could make use of a high-power atomizer in his laboratory. One thing was crystal clear: I was overlooking somebody.

Pling! My laptop announced that I had mail after finally having booted up. There were two chain letters against military intervention in Iraq that I was supposed to sign and distribute further, and the usual foolproof investment advice explaining why this was the right time to invest in a time-share on the Mediterranean, container ships on the Atlantic, and a most promising diamond mine in Africa. Somehow the Internet had long ago identified me as a doctor, and doctors are richer than Croesus, everybody knows that. Even some company called Alpha Pharmaceuticals seemed to know that. The subject line of its e-mail was regarding a new antibiotic. One that I'd never heard of, which was strange. As a doctor, you usually hear what's in the pipeline. That was the only reason I didn't trash the message at once along with the others.

As soon as I'd opened the message, I could tell it wasn't from a real pharmaceutical company. The more I read, the more excited I got. Was I jumping to conclusions? Was I shaping the world according to my desires? I urgently needed help on this. Someone had to help me figure out what this e-mail was really trying to tell me. And who had sent it. And from where. Or if somebody was cruelly pulling my leg.

I copied the surprisingly large dataset onto a thumb drive, put it in my pocket, and hurried to my car. I had to see someone with some computer literacy fast.

Nobody had to remind me that my go-to computer expert would normally have been Celine, the academic mathematician. I knew life would go on without her, but it was still hard.

Driving well over the speed limit, I headed over to Michael's laboratory, where I was sure I would find him still working away. Michael didn't have a theoretical background in computers like Celine, but you had to be a pretty good electrical engineer to run an analytic lab these days. Besides, computers and the Internet were Michael's hobbies, in addition to silk ties, excellent food, and good-looking lab assistants. In short, he knew less about computers than Celine, but a hell of a lot more than me.

"Felix! What's new?"

Michael's "What's new?" was as much a part of him as his classy silk ties and the good mood with which he welcomed me at this late hour. As was the question that followed—"What can I do for you?"—which I knew was entirely sincere. I just wished that I had a positive reply to his "What's new?" and that some day in the future his "What can I do for you?" would be fully answered by "Just open a couple of beers for us," as it had been before Celine's disappearance.

I gave him a short rundown of everyone who had asked about the missing "water purification plant."

"I bet you Herr Sommer took it and found some other way to get it to his Iraqi friends," Michael suggested.

But that was the least of my concerns at the moment. I stuck my thumb drive under his nose.

"Michael! I think Celine is alive!"

As a doctor, I knew all too well the look that Michael shot my way. He was looking for other signs of my madness, which, due to our friendship, had evaded him before. But either Michael didn't find them or didn't want to further excite his clearly lunatic friend. Either way, he put forward one of his practical suggestions.

"Let me start by getting us a beer. Then you can tell me what this is all about, step by step. And convince me, I hope. How does that sound?"

While Michael went to get our drinks, I uploaded my e-mail from Alpha Pharmaceuticals onto his computer. Something he normally would have killed me for, regardless of his automatic virus-search program. By the time he popped the caps off the bottles, the message had opened.

"So what? I've never heard of Alpha Pharmaceuticals either, but you can't possibly know every last company. You know yourself what a lively trade there is in e-mail addresses on the Internet. You get them for every target group, based on occupation, monthly income, even shoe size, for all I know."

"That's not the point, Michael. Just read the text and look at the pictures."

This company, Alpha Pharmaceuticals, had just developed a new, allegedly superpotent antibiotic they called Stegamycin. According to their message, this Stegamycin was the best bacteria killer ever, and bad news for any infectious little bugger out there. But if I wasn't totally off the mark, the future didn't look entirely bleak for bacteria and associates.

"Why does this name bother you so much, Felix? Vibramycin, streptomycin, vancomycin, all of them are potent antibiotics. Why shouldn't they name their new antibiotic Stegamycin? Sounds good to me."

I was getting more and more wound up, by then almost completely certain about my theory.

"Michael, for God's sake, I told you to look at the pictures! Why, of all things, would there be a picture of a shell?"

"The text says they extract their Stegamycin from this shell. Makes sense to me."

But Michael finally caught on.

"Hey, you're right. They should shoot their marketing personnel. That's a pretty stupid mistake they made with the name."

"That's what I mean, Michael. I don't believe it's a mistake. A company that produces antibiotics surely knows the difference between shells and fungi."

For anybody in the medical field, it was easy to see what I was getting at. Many antibiotics are extracted from fungi, which is why their name ends in *mycin*, after the Latin word for mushrooms, *mycetes*. But *mycin* didn't fit at all for a pill that was allegedly extracted from some kind of shell.

"Well, let's take a look at this questionable firm," Michael said as he typed Alpha Pharmaceuticals into his laptop. But Google couldn't find the firm producing this revolutionary bacteria killer, nor could Yahoo or any of those other übersmart search engines.

Even so, Michael wasn't fully convinced of my sanity yet. And rightly so. So far, we only had an unknown pharmaceutical firm that had my e-mail address but no Internet presence, and which had given an absurd name to their product. It was strange, granted, but not much more than that.

"OK. But where's your link to Celine? You've got something more, don't you?"

Yes, there was something more. Because neither the pharmaceutical firm nor the absurdly named antibiotic had initially caught my attention. It was the picture of the shell that had alarmed me.

"This shell is called *Cytherea meretrix*, Michael. And I know three things about this shell. One, its natural habitat is the South Pacific; two, you don't produce antibiotics from it; and three, I myself buried about a hundred of them in the soil of the Spreewald outside Berlin two years ago for Celine to find. Where she found them, while out on a walk with Beate. It's a little private joke of ours."

"*Cytherea matrix*?"

"*Cytherea meretrix*, or prickly Venus clam. I found that described Celine nicely. Aside from mussels, these are pretty much the only shell I know by name."

Michael still looked at me with some concern, but he probably thought that I couldn't be entirely out of my mind if I could handle the shell's complicated name. And, though he knew that lunatics sometimes show surprising intellectual capacities, he wanted to be convinced. After all, this was about Celine.

"Jeez, Felix! You really think that's possible? Pour that beer down the sink. Champagne on the house!"

It was a long, totally amped-up night. After the first bottle of champagne, Michael agreed that this was almost certainly a message from Celine. Who else would think of some South Pacific shell that we shared a history with? While several different decryption tools scanned the message, two no-longer-truly-young men performed ritual dances in the high-tech lab. Our activities were later reinforced by a younger woman, as Michael had the good idea to call Beate and get her out of bed.

"Take a cab, or a chopper, Beate. Trust me, you don't want to miss this!"

An hour later, though, disillusionment began to set in. None of Michael's decryption tools had given us any leads. We read and reread the message. Suddenly, Michael slapped his forehead.

"God, are we dumb! It's just that Celine apparently has no idea just *how* dumb we are!"

Though Beate and I didn't entirely agree with him, he got our full attention with his remark.

"The key to this is not in the text. We could analyze this text for a hundred more hours and still not get any further. It's in the name Stegamycin! *That's* the key!"

Had Michael had too much to drink? Had too much blood drained from his brain from our ritual dances? We'd already tried the term *Stegamycin*, and different variations of it, about a thousand times as the keyword in the decryption process, to no avail.

"No, you dummies! Not as the access key. Felix has already realized that the suffix *-mycin* is a lead, because a shell isn't a mushroom. The same is true for first syllable, the *stega* part! Have you never heard of steganography?"

Beate and I exchanged baffled looks. No, we hadn't. Michael enlightened us.

"Steganography is a technique that involves hiding a message in a picture. It's actually nothing new, but it's become highly refined in the digital age. And not so hard to decipher once you know it's steganography and what picture to work on."

"The shell!"

The rest was surprisingly easy. Looking for *steganography* on the Internet, Michael quickly found a decryption tool with the telling name Steganos. The correct keyword turned out to be *Spreewald*, which was where I had buried the shells for Celine.

After a few more minutes, we could finally read her message:

"Hope to be back with you all soon."

"With you all." Of course Celine would have known that I would need help deciphering her message!

"Why doesn't she say where she is? And how she plans to get out of wherever that is?" Beate moaned.

Perhaps because there was no more champagne.

"Because Celine is a careful girl," Michael said. "We're not the only people in this world who can read encrypted e-mails."

"But there must be a way to find out where that message came from!"

"Yes and no," Michael explained. "I already checked. This message came to us from Moscow. Or, rather, from a server there. And the only reason this server exists is to make it impossible for us to find out where the e-mail really originated."

"I'm not sure I understand. What are servers like that good for?"

"Precisely what Celine used it for. These servers do exactly what they claim to: they serve. They serve people or organizations that do not want their illegal chain letters to be tracked back to their sender. They're used for blackmail, child pornography, to anonymously warn against assassinations or terrorist attacks. Thousands of things. That's why our various governments don't shut them down. They're useful."

Well after midnight, we finally called it a day. We were pretty sure that Celine was alive and would be back with us again soon. I was beyond happy. I was elated.

Partly as a result of the champagne, Beate and I finally slept together that night. But as any psychologist would have pointed out, alcohol as a rule doesn't make you do things you don't want to do but simply catalyzes actions that would have happened sooner or later anyway. What a feast it would have been for a psychologist to explain why it happened that night.

CHAPTER 24

The morning after: disillusionment. I was wrung out in every sense of the word. Some blood alcohol, less testosterone. That and a thousand known and yet unknown biological mechanisms and regulatory circuits ensured that the skeptics held the upper hand at that morning's cerebral roundtable discussion, while, a little farther down, I brushed my teeth. Was that e-mail really from Celine? Was the picture of *Cytherea meretrix* really enough proof of that? The story of the South Pacific shells buried in the Spreewald might have been beaten out of her. Or Celine could have told her friend Heiner about it at some point during their long journey, and it had been beaten out of him. Maybe beating it out of him hadn't even been necessary.

If that was the case, what did the message mean? Who would want to make me believe that Celine was still alive, and why? And if Celine really was alive, why were the Iraqis spreading the story about her having been a victim of her own bombing attack?

Next question: If Celine was alive, what about the coffin from Baghdad? Or rather, what did it contain? Who or what had we buried? Certain officials in Germany must know the answer, as there was no way that coffin hadn't been opened. But I doubted those officials would give me any information.

Several phone calls later, it was clear that it would be easier to get permission for Celine's exhumation than to get the "import papers" for her coffin. To have a look at those papers, I'd have to find out who was sitting on them and how to get an order to surrender them. Getting exhumation permission was less ambiguous, as you just needed to get a court order. I could try to get one myself, but I knew that a request from Celine's parents would have a better chance of success.

Which is why I found myself on the autobahn driving toward Hamburg late that afternoon. By early evening, I was parked in front of their row house in Hamburg-Bergedorf. The sun had set, but it wasn't dark yet. The light over the front door had already been turned on.

"Is that you, Felix Hoffmann?" Celine's father asked. He was squinting, his glasses hanging on a chain around his neck. "What do you want?"

"It's about Celine."

His first impulse, it seemed, was to shut the door in my face. But then he opened it a little further and headed back inside without a word. I followed him into the living room, where he pointed to a chair. I sat down.

"I'll go get her mother."

I looked around. Aside from the lack of a decorated fir tree, the room looked unchanged since Celine and I had fled that Christmas many years ago. But if these people had a Christmas tree every year—which I doubted—not a thing would have to be moved. Its spot, a little to the right of the open fireplace, remained empty. There were signs of stagnation everywhere. The people who lived there were done living their lives, the room told me. They might not have known it themselves yet, but the room knew. It occurred to me once again that they were only a little more than ten years older than me. Would that be my lot in ten years, too?

The pair finally descended from the second floor. I had no idea what had taken them so long. I told them why I had come.

"No. Absolutely not!"

Herr Bergkamp had taken his wife's hand, which she seemed unaware of as she continued working on a crumpled-up Kleenex. Hadn't they heard me? Hadn't they understood? I told them about the e-mail all over again, about the shell and the encrypted message.

"Do you hear me? I'm telling you that your daughter is probably alive! And even if I'm wrong, don't you want to know for sure?"

"Felix, this is final. There will be no exhumation."

I jumped from my chair.

"You didn't bury your daughter in that cemetery. You'd already buried her when she went to Iraq against your will. Or maybe even years before that, when we left you alone with your Christmas goose."

Celine's father was about to say something, but his wife stopped him. I sat back down, waiting. By then it was dark outside and we were sitting in near darkness. They still hadn't offered me so much as a cup of coffee.

Something felt totally wrong. Could it be that I was totally wrong? Shouldn't her parents have acted overjoyed when I told them that their daughter might well be alive? Shouldn't they be asking me all kinds of questions, alternating between the fear of being hurt again and wanting to believe that what I thought or hoped might in fact be possible? But the only feeling they conveyed to me was some kind of superior knowledge. And that not only I, but my revelations, were not really welcome. What did these people know that I didn't?

Slowly it all added up: the absence of joy over what I had told them, the absence of real mourning, the absence of photos of their daughter around the house. And I finally realized why they hadn't emptied Celine's apartment in Berlin.

"You've known all along!"

Telling silence.

"Am I the only one you didn't tell? Did all your has-been revolutionaries at the cemetery know? Did you all have a good laugh at me afterward?"

"It's got nothing to do with you, Felix. We were told this was the best way. For Celine. We did it for Celine. And no, we were the only ones who knew at the funeral."

I began to understand.

"For Celine? Really? Or 'in the best interest of the Federal Republic of Germany'? I can't believe it! What would you do today if there were someone from the Red Army Faction knocking at your door again? Let the dogs loose? Or call your friends from the Verfassungsschutz?"

With hurt feelings and certain of my moral superiority, I left the pair sitting alone in their dark row house, got in my car, and started searching for the entrance to the autobahn back to Berlin.

Traffic was light, and the two-hundred-mile drive gave me enough time to tend to my feelings. I had been deceived, betrayed, and taken for a fool. I punched the steering wheel. I was angry at Celine's parents, yes, but also angry at myself, for I had always felt that I wasn't mourning Celine sufficiently. Or was I angry about having lost the feeling of loss?

It wasn't until I was stuck in a traffic jam due to an accident around Neuruppin that I asked myself what I would have done in Celine's parents' place. Had they really been wrong to cooperate with the Verfassungsschutz? Wasn't I just angry that they had trusted people like Jablonske and Waldeck more than me?

Because none of this was about me, I wasn't in any danger, or, if I was, only because of the death wish that was apparently pervasive in German drivers on the autobahn. But this was a case of a woman in a country where the term *civil rights* was unknown and where no humanitarian organization would ever be allowed to visit the prisons. In that situation, I, too, probably wouldn't have entrusted my daughter's life to Dr. Hoffmann. Just as this Dr. Hoffmann would not share his latest findings with his good friends Beate and Michael.

By the time the traffic jam started to dissolve, I had quieted down considerably. The casualties had been sped away to the nearest hospital, their totaled cars hauled off the road. Like everybody else, I ogled the crash site, still illuminated by rotating blue flashing lights. And like everybody else, I was relieved not to have been buried in any of those smashed-up cars myself. Even if she was alive, I felt that Celine had indeed been buried in a sense. Buried by Dr. Hoffmann, when he slept with her best friend the night before. At the very moment that Celine had reported she was alive.

I finally reached the outskirts of Berlin. I had felt distinctly better a few hours earlier, when I'd left Hamburg in a position of moral superiority.

CHAPTER 25

By three in the morning I was back home, which gave me three hours to sleep. Much to my surprise, I actually slept and even felt well rested when I had to get up. I felt rather proud of how well I was functioning when I entered the conference room of the internal medicine department, just in time for our morning conference.

But something was very wrong there. Nobody else had shown up for our usual morning routine of haggling about CT time, empty beds, and nurses who had called in sick. What was going on? Had the plague really broken out? Another terrorism exercise? Or was there are a case of real terrorism this time? Was the hospital cut off from the world and surrounded by snipers? I looked out the window. Aside from the a few empty spaces in the employee parking lot, everything looked normal to me.

I called my ward.

"This is Hoffmann. What's going on? What have I missed?"

"I'm not allowed to give you any information regarding our patients over the phone."

Wonderful! I was talking to one of our student nurses. I knew that explanations and further questions would only confuse her. I stormed over to internal medicine, where I ran into nurse Käthe.

"Dr. Hoffmann! What are you doing here so early on a weekend!?"

"What day is it today, Käthe?"

"Saturday. Spaghetti day!"

OK, I might have been functioning, but apparently I had to allow for a certain margin of error.

Since I was there, I wondered what would be the best use of my time. If I looked in on my patients, I would just get in the way of the nurses. I decided to go check on our supplies in the basement again. Who knew what I might find. But, of course, Sommer's atomizer had not magically reappeared, and even under torture I still couldn't have told any interested party where it was. The question would come up again, I was sure.

Perhaps it was the thought of torture that brought Dr. Hassan to mind. I decided I should talk to him again. At that point, I was pretty sure that I'd be speaking directly to the Iraqi secret police through him. But I was informed that Dr. Hassan was not at the hospital that weekend. It would have to wait until Monday then—unless I went directly to his bosses at the embassy.

After seeing a few patients, I put my feet up on my desk in my office and let my mind wander while my workstation was warming up. I thought of another Saturday morning, one with Celine in a little hotel in the Spreewald, where we had been woken up to clucking chickens and the smell of freshly brewed coffee. There were no new messages from Celine or Alpha Pharmaceuticals. Without great enthusiasm, I went to work compiling the long-overdue quality reports and other department statistics that were such an important part of a doctor's job these days—and as good a way as any to spend a Saturday.

That evening, I was alone at home when Michael called.

"Hello, Felix! What's new?"

Well, actually a few things were new since we had last spoken. I had slept with Celine's best friend and yelled at her already-frightened parents, for example.

I muttered something unintelligible into the phone, which Michael apparently interpreted as a signal that the line might be tapped, and he acted accordingly.

"Listen, Felix. It's about the message from those shell collectors we talked about the other day. You can delete it now, OK?"

"OK, Michael. I'll do that."

I was sure Michael had his reasons for wanting me to delete that message from Alpha Pharmaceuticals. Michael knew that I didn't download my e-mails via Outlook Express like most people but rather directly from my provider. Unlike Celine, I didn't suspect a worldwide conspiracy every time a journalist was killed in a car accident or somebody from Greenpeace fell off a ladder while painting his house, but I shared a general suspicion about Microsoft's products and privacy issues.

When I opened my mailbox at gmx.de, I found that somebody else had already taken care of it. The e-mail from Alpha Pharmaceuticals was gone.

Later that night, my phone rang, but I didn't answer. I thought it might be Beate, and I didn't have any idea what to say to her yet.

CHAPTER 26

I was indecisive and moody for the remainder of the weekend. Indecisive about whether I should let Michael and Beate in on my visit to Celine's parents and my new plan. And moody about how to handle what had taken place between Beate and myself. Lying awake beside her on the morning after, I had thought of a suitable line or two. But after my first mumbled words, Beate had put a finger over my lips.

"Shush. Don't get all worked up about this. You just looked like you needed it."

Dr. Hoffmann, a sexual welfare recipient? A social case at the mercy of our CEO? That didn't quite fit my self-perception. I decided that a beer with Michael would lift my spirits.

We met at the Waldhaus and instantly found ourselves in the midst of a melange of beer, cigarette smoke, and humanity that you just can't recreate with any authenticity at home.

"Felix, did you delete the e-mail like I told you to?"

"I didn't need to. Somebody else had already taken care of it."

"Huh? Are you sure you didn't delete it on Thursday night, after you'd copied it onto your thumb drive?"

I was pretty sure I hadn't. But then, after my Saturday morning visit to Berlin South the day before, I wouldn't have bet on it.

"Could be," Michael continued, "that our smart Celine sent it with a built-in self-destruction mechanism, one of those 'burn after reading' things."

"I always thought stuff like that only worked on *Mission: Impossible*."

Michael scanned the room with exaggerated care and leaned in toward me.

"I just hope you're referring to the movie and not the TV series we used to watch together. That was on twenty years ago!"

No need for me to admit that I had indeed been thinking of the TV series. Michael remained in his conspirative posture.

"By the way, Dr. Hoffmann, how was your night with Beate?"

"What makes you think we spent the night together?"

"C'mon. It was written all over your face when you left that night. And Beate's, too. Plain for everybody to see."

Interesting. I hadn't seen it.

"And it was the last chance for the two of you before Celine is back. So how was it?"

I truthfully reported Beate's remarks from the morning after, which caused Michael, who had just taken a sip of his beer, to almost choke to death from laughter. He sprayed half of his beer onto my face.

"'You just looked like you needed it! That's what she said? Wonderful! You have to teach me that look, Felix!'"

Now I had to laugh, too, and I ordered another round of beers. As often happened when I was with Michael, I began to believe that life may not really be as complicated as I always thought it was.

CHAPTER 27

There were times when I didn't run into Beate in the hospital for a whole week, but I almost ran right into her in the lobby on Monday. At the last moment, I jumped into the elevator. Beate seemed to be everywhere that morning, and I got very adept at taking sudden turns. One of those turns ended up costing me an extra half hour when I landed in our prenatal clinic, where my colleagues thanked me for coming to see their patient so quickly. In an effort to avoid the cafeteria, I had to ask nurse Käthe to bring me lunch. But finally, in the early afternoon, it happened. In the corridor leading to intensive care, there was no turn I could take.

"Hi, Felix. You're not trying to avoid me, are you? I missed our Sunday dinner last night!"

"Weren't you at that conference with all the Vitalis CEOs?"

"That was a week ago, my friend. We even talked about it then."

So I admitted to her that I wasn't sure how to talk to her since our night together, what our situation was, or whether there even was a situation. And how that night fit with both of us being so happy that Celine hopefully was on her way back.

Beate looked around, made sure we were alone, and then gave me a quick kiss.

"Oh Felix, you're so old-fashioned. It's so sweet! Don't worry, you and Celine are a perfect match—for people like yourselves, at least. I would never think of getting between you. And I don't feel like I've betrayed my best friend, really."

What more could I wish for? Listening to Beate crying on my voice mail every night? Or suddenly standing at my door with her toothbrush and suitcase? But then, wasn't she being a little too cool about this? That's the trouble with people like me, the ones who've never really matured into full adults: no matter what happens, they're never entirely comfortable.

"So, Felix, no need to be afraid of me. Let's go get a cup of coffee, because there are a few things from that CEO conference we have to talk about. And we still need to figure out what we can do to learn more about Celine's whereabouts."

We went to what was still my department-head office, which had the luxury of having an old coffee machine. Beate had a super-fancy Italian one, but the size of her CEO office always intimidated me a bit, as did the wooden African dancers on her desk.

"So what was new at the conference?"

"The first point of order was security. How do we keep bums, lunatics, and terrorists out of here? I told them our plan for that was ready anytime."

I remembered that Beate had asked me to work on that plan. That had been before our plague exercise, and I had since forgotten all about it. To this day, anybody could wander in there unaccosted, or, for that matter, carry out a water purification plant—rather, some heavy-duty atomizer. I hated to think what could be brought in!

"I'll get to work on that right away."

Beate gave me a questioning look, so I elaborated.

"Well, I'll find somebody to get to work on it."

"The big issue at the conference though was time management again. You know, optimizing our work processes. I'm afraid that we'll have those ladies and gentlemen with stopwatches stepping on our toes here before long."

Great. In the end, I would know on a statistical level just how often I went to the bathroom, and whether I needed to be concerned about it. But it might be interesting to learn how much unpaid overtime we all did.

"What about patient-doctor relationships? Did they talk about how they want to ensure confidentiality?"

"Yes, they hadn't thought that through yet, which is why we have a little grace period. In the end, I imagine they'll just add something about it in small print to the forms the patients have to sign. Nobody reads those forms anyway."

I nodded, not really paying attention. I knew we would get around to talking about Celine soon, and I wasn't yet sure how much to tell Beate. When the time came, I felt I should at least tell her about my visit to her parents, and what I had found out from them. Perhaps it was just her perfume, but I thought she had a right to know.

She put her arms around me.

"Felix, she wasn't in that coffin! We never buried her! We'll throw a gigantic party when Celine comes back. Put that stupid funeral behind us. Party for a whole week!"

Maybe it was that simple and I was just an old pessimist who refused to understand that everything was going to be all right in the end.

Well, maybe not everything. Beate had one more thing to tell me from her conference.

"You haven't asked me if we talked about the department-head position."

Right, I hadn't. It wasn't a priority at the moment. I knew that I wasn't a top contender, since I hadn't been among the candidates invited to interview for the position. I probably wasn't on the list at all if Sommer had kept his word.

"At the moment, this is where it stands: Candidates number one and two have already declined; they didn't like the small print. Especially the percentage of private patients' fees they were expected to hand over to Vitalis. But the Vitalis people hinted, on the down-low, that you're not necessarily any further up the ladder. Word has come from the health department that they don't want to see you as department head. Not after that press conference."

So it wasn't my friend Sommer. Another fine example of how our local government and the supposedly private Vitalis Group were in bed together. I wasn't especially disappointed, because deep down I had never really wanted to become department head. I had entered the race mainly to test my market value and for the fun of turning down the offer if it came. On the plus side, I knew that after that press conference, Zentis wouldn't be getting the job either. At least that was a certainty, wasn't it?

Berlin Station, Progress Report (ref. III-77-1414)

Subject: Dr. Felix Hoffmann
From: Agent McGilly, Agent Thorne
Source of information: personal interview and follow-up observation

Summary: The subject was interviewed by agents McGilly and Thorne at his private residence (apartment) in Berlin. The agents identified themselves as US government officials. The subject didn't seem overly surprised that he had been contacted by us and agreed to talk. He did not deny his connection to Mr. Sommer (ref. III-76-1391), but insisted on the exclusively business nature of this relationship. He referred to the object in question as a "water purification plant" and denied any knowledge of its present whereabouts. About thirty minutes after the interview, Hoffmann emerged from his apartment, clearly agitated, and left in his car, traveling well above the speed limit. Due to a breakdown in communication between Agent McGilly and Agent Thorne, Hoffmann was lost before reaching his destination, which remains unknown.

Assessment: The information volunteered by the suspect is not plausible. His contacts to suspect Sommer clearly go beyond what he admitted, e.g., their dinner at the restaurant Trenta Sei (in Gendarmenmarkt, see photos in the addendum). Furthermore, Hoffmann has been in direct contact with the Iraqi intelligence service (ref. III-77-1411), as has suspect Sommer. It is highly improbable that Hoffmann does not know the current location of the object in question.

Furthermore, Hoffman exhibits some clearly conspirative and/or suspicious behavior:

1. Unlike before, he has taken to parking his car in different locations at a considerable distance from his address.
2. Our interview clearly agitated him, which was only revealed after the fact.
3. He most likely reported our interview at once to a third party (Sommer?).

Suggested further action: 24/7 surveillance of the suspect is again urgently recommended. Disclosure of our findings to German authorities is again strongly discouraged.

PS: This was, despite repeated repairs, the third communication breakdown in a single month. We urgently need new cell phones! Handwritten on printout:

1. Chuck, what's wrong with the damn cell phones? Why can't we just buy new ones?
2. Where the hell is our "object of interest"? Sure this Hoffmann knows! What kind of leverage do we have on this guy?

Bundesamt für Verfassungsschutz
Dept. IV, File #286-03

Subject: Celine Ulrike Bergkamp

The Foreign Office still has no reliable information on the whereabouts of subject Celine Ulrike Bergkamp, either from sources inside Iraq or from our acting embassy in Amman. DNA taken from the corpse inside the coffin sent from Baghdad is definitively not from the suspect (DNA from the suspect was taken from a hair comb provided by her parents). According to the Foreign Office, Iraqi officials still maintain that the suspect died in a self-imposed bomb attack. It is now almost certain that this is a myth. Given the circumstances, this office is almost certain that subject Bergkamp is alive and most likely undergoing (further?) schooling in terrorist techniques and tactics in Iraq and/or Syria.

This assumption is strongly supported by the documented activities of the subject in so-called human rights groups and her part in militant actions within these circles. Furthermore, the subject has been raised in this sort of environment: Although her parents are cooperating at the moment, they have a history of supporting the Red Army Faction.

Intensification of schooling of foreign nationals in terrorist techniques and tactics in Iraq must be seen as a direct consequence of the hitherto denied, now apparently proven, cooperation between Saddam Hussein and al-Qaida, as reported by high-level US sources in recent months.

Disclosure of our findings to BND is not recommended: The BND is only responsible for activities outside of Germany. The subject's actions have so far only taken place in Germany, and the subject's target of terrorist action also appears to be Germany.

Cross-references: subject Felix Hoffmann, MD, subject Heiner Schmidt, US State Department
[Signature illegible]
Bundesamt für Verfassungsschutz
Technological Department
Circular note to all departments
Ref: electronic mail (e-mail)

In monitoring e-mail traffic, e-mails from or to suspects have at times been deleted lately. This is unacceptable, all the more so because there have been cases when e-mails have been irretrievably destroyed before they were even analyzed. Fixing the problem is the department's highest priority. Until further notice, employing the utmost diligence with monitored e-mail traffic is recommended.

Bundesamt für Verfassungsschutz
Legal Department
Circular note to all departments
Ref: legal basis for monitoring telecommunication (update and refresher)

In light of recent events we want to make all concerned aware once again of the legal basis for monitoring conventional mail and telecommunication services (e-mail, Internet). Some Internet providers (hereafter: providers) are still uncooperative and unaware of their legal obligation to provide us with complete access to all the telecommunication activities of their subjects. In particular, they often do not meet their legal obligation to provide an interface for direct monitoring of telecommunication activities.

Providers that are found to be uncooperative should be urgently reminded of the relevant legal provisions, which are: Strafprozeßordnung § 99, 100 a, 100 b (in der Fassung der Bekanntmachung vom 7. April 1987 (BGBl. I S. 1047, 1319), zuletzt geändert durch Artikel 2 Abs. 14 des Gesetzes vom 17. Dezember 1997 (BGBl. I S. 3039), Außenwirtschaftsgesetz § 39, Bundesdatenschutzgesetz vom 20. Dezember 1990 (BGBl. I S. 2954), zuletzt geändert durch Artikel 3 des Gesetzes vom 16. Dezember 1997 (BGBl. I S. 3094), Strafgesetzbuch § 88, 202 ff, in der Fassung der Bekanntmachung vom 10. März 1987 (BGBl. I S. 945, 1160), zuletzt geändert durch Artikel 14 § 16 des Gesetzes vom 16. Dezember 1997 (BGBl. I S. 2942), Strafgesetzbuch § 138, Gesetz zu Artikel zehn GG (Begleitgesetz zum Telekommunikationsgesetz (BegleitG) vom 17. Dezember 1997).

CHAPTER 28

It happened a few days later. And only when it was over did I remember that Beate had warned me. Two things in particular angered me: that I hadn't taken her warning seriously and that it happened right in front of my door. Sure, it was pretty late when I came home from the hospital and, because it was late February, it was dark already. But didn't my attackers worry that somebody would be watching from a window or walking by with a dog? Or that someone would come to help me? Hadn't I just seen a curtain being opened? It probably just happened too fast, even though it seemed to me like hours passed before they stopped beating me on the stomach and head.

When my attackers didn't accept my friendly offer—that they "just take my wallet and get lost!"—I started to think that I was being subjected to some kind of pedagogic measure. Which proved to be correct when those assholes made sure that I understood what the lesson they were teaching me was about.

"This is to teach you not to steal what's not yours, Herr Doctor!"

This well-meant reminder was underscored with a final kick in the butt.

There was a third thing that made me angry: the leader of the gang had made no attempt to hide his identity, though he surely must have known I would recognize him. But then, how else would I have known who to thank for that misguided reminder of right and wrong?

A little later, after I'd helped myself to some iodine tincture, a glass of chardonnay, and two aspirin, I analyzed the situation. I came up with two top-priority issues: Who else might decide to actively jump-start my memory regarding the location of that water-purification–poison-gas apparatus? And, more important, how could I help Celine, who I was convinced was alive?

I'd actually been thinking how I—or we—could help Celine when I ran into these goons. Again my usual parking spot in front of the building was occupied, this time by a TV repair truck. Was there really nothing we could do but wait for Celine to suddenly reappear? Who could possibly help us? Some government agency perhaps?

So far, the German government hadn't proved very helpful. At least to my knowledge. Had they perhaps made some deal with Celine's parents? But I knew her parents wouldn't tell me if that were the case, even if I paid them another visit. So what were our options? To try to alert the press? That might put some pressure on the German government, but it surely would leave the Iraqis unimpressed, given that even a multitude of UN resolutions didn't seem to make much of an impression on them. Then there was the question of whether any given action might be counterproductive, putting Celine in even more danger. If she wasn't rotting away in some Iraqi prison, she must be in hiding somewhere, or trying to get out of the country. Would our taking action—like engaging the press—only cause the Iraqis to look harder for her? The more I thought about it, the less I knew what to do.

As I'd expected, a concerned Herr Sommer called me at the hospital the next day. He'd heard that I'd been in an accident, he said.

"I am sure, Dr. Hoffmann, that with a little cooperation from you, nothing like that will happen again."

Did he pull that line from some second-rate crime movie? Or did those movies actually draw from reality? I thought a cunning answer was called for, but none came to mind. I was still brooding about when and from whom I should expect the next attack.

"Just instruct your Mr. Sobotka to stay away from me."

I slammed down the receiver.

What could I do? Move to Celine's apartment? Or even move to Beate's? No, I could still be tracked down at the hospital. Further disciplinary measures could easily be inflicted in the employee parking lot, for instance. Hadn't I better just disappear altogether for a while? Take a little vacation?

"What are you talking about, Felix? Are you nuts?"

I thought that Beate was referring to the clinic, reminding me that I was acting department head.

"First of all, Beate, I still have all these vacations days. Second, I'm never going to become department head, so why should I work myself to death for Vitalis? And third, there's still Professor Kleinweg, our official acting department head."

"Yeah, I'm sure he'd love that. Regardless, I'm not talking about the hospital."

I finally understood what she was referring to. Yes, Beate was worried about keeping the hospital running in my absence, but she was more concerned about the destination I had in mind: Iraq.

CHAPTER 29

Was a trip to Iraq really a crackpot idea, perhaps an effect of having been hit on the head a little too hard by Herr Sommer's goons, as Michael suggested? Maybe so, but the more Michael and Beate tried to talk me out of going, the more I became set on it.

"Do you really think that sitting around here and waiting to see who's going to beat me up next is a more attractive idea? I might as well get beaten up in Iraq."

"And do you think that Saddam's henchmen will confine themselves to a little light bashing when they get hold of a nonbeliever who's nosing around in their country looking for his girlfriend who's been throwing bombs at them or helping the Kurds, or both?"

Michael had a point, as did Beate: "Going to Iraq isn't crazy. But your guilty conscience after we slept together is. Whether or not you're aware of it, this trip is your way of doing penance so that you can wash that night off your conscience. Only this time it's not a walk to Canossa, but to Baghdad."

Beate and Michael came up with more arguments, among them the growing possibility of the Americans going to war against Iraq. But I stuck to my plan, convinced that this was exactly what I should have done in the first place. It seemed the only way to get clarification on what had happened, what was going on, and how to help Celine effectively. Besides, I had all those brochures I'd been given at the embassy—didn't they amount to a direct invitation?

The trip required some preparation, but that wouldn't take long. First, I moved into Celine's apartment. Which was no big deal, as I still had a toothbrush and some other stuff there. Although the apartment was, as I've pointed out before, just across the street, it had a big advantage over mine: the entrance was around the corner and not visible to anyone with questionable intentions who might be waiting for me at my own front door.

Beate and Michael were the only ones who knew my real destination; everyone else thought I was bound for Egypt to do a bit of sunbathing and snorkeling in the Red Sea. I booked my Berlin–Frankfurt–Cairo flight at a nearby travel agency, then used Michael's Visa card to purchase the remainder of the trip—Cairo–Damascus–Baghdad—on the Internet. I knew from the embassy brochures that I needed a current HIV test to be admitted to Iraq. I also needed either an official invitation from an Iraqi citizen or a visa from the embassy. The HIV test was negative, which I had expected yet was still relieved to see. But I neither wanted to file officially for a visa—because any application would surely be checked by the Iraqi secret police—nor to ask our Dr. Hassan for an invitation from his family, which, I was certain, would have the same effect.

Instead I counted on the power of dollars and euros in a country whose citizens were on the edge of starvation due to the international embargo. Furthermore, due to increasingly militant statements from Washington, there was already a growing tourism to Baghdad of "human shields." I wasn't planning to be part of that shield, but the concept might shield my entrance to the country.

CHAPTER 30

"You can't do this to me! This is highly unprofessional!"

I wasn't surprised by the lack of enthusiasm with which Professor Kleinweg reacted to the news of my vacation. However, my sympathy for him was limited. I was effectively doing his job at Berlin South, which included all the private patients he billed. It was about time, I thought, that he worked a little for his money.

"I am truly sorry for the inconvenience this is causing you, Herr Kleinweg. But if I don't use my vacation days from last year now, I'll lose them."

"Really, Herr Hoffmann, I am sure this can be worked out somehow. You know, I could understand your suddenly deciding to go off on vacation if it had something to do with your dead girlfriend. But sunbathing in Egypt! That's much too dangerous right now. It's all Arabs there, too. You might as well go to Iraq!"

I suppressed a smile.

It was time for Thursday rounds with Kleinweg, who was not amused that he really had to pay attention, even take notes. That was not his idea of what an "acting department head" did.

"I must make one thing absolutely clear, Herr Hoffmann: I won't have the time to supervise the dialysis patients in addition to the others. Do you have any idea how to handle that?"

This had nothing to do with the additional workload, and everything to do with his competence in this area. Or rather, incompetence. And just as both of us knew that, we both knew that Kleinweg would never admit it.

"We have a visiting doctor from Iraq. He's very good with the kidney machines. I don't foresee any problems there."

Kleinweg relaxed. It seemed to me that a little dampener was in order. "Of course, I'm sure he'll have a question from time to time."

Or might just vanish one day altogether, I thought. But I didn't want to make Kleinweg any more nervous than he already was. However, I found it remarkable that I hadn't heard anything more about Hassan's brother-in-law's trucking company after Hassan learned that a certain item was missing from the second shipment.

CHAPTER 31

My flight to Baghdad would involve layovers and plane changes in Frankfurt, Cairo, and Damascus, which meant at least three chances for checked baggage to get lost. I was sure that if I ever got to Baghdad, I would have bigger problems to solve than filling out lost-luggage forms. Which is why I limited myself to what would fit into Celine's carry-on bag. I also threw in her map of Iraq and some antibiotics and diarrhea medication. Although I wasn't expecting to be invited to any fancy dinners there, the clothes I'd kept at Celine's place weren't sufficient. I had to go back to my place.

It was raining cats and dogs when I decided to head over there. Actually, the entire zoo seemed to be coming down. Which didn't mean that I had to get wet. Back in World War II, people in Berlin waited out air raids in their cellars. But if the house above them collapsed, they were trapped. So, as was the case with many of the buildings from that period, all the houses on the block were connected by tunnels, to give people a chance to escape from their cellars if their house was hit.

As a result, I discovered that the door to my cellar had been broken down only because of the rain and my desire not to get wet. And because I was already on high alert, I also noticed that the lock to my front door had been tampered with. I was also quite certain that the chaotic state in which I found my place wasn't the result of my own sloppiness, but rather, inflicted by some pretty ruthless search.

Searching for what? The atomizer, of course. And after they didn't unearth it in my cellar, they had looked for some clues to its whereabouts up there. But who? Sommer's people? Or had somebody else gotten nosy? In any case, it was another argument in favor of disappearing for a while, and Iraq was surely a good place to do just that. As long as I didn't disappear for good.

I grabbed some underwear, socks, T-shirts, and a pair of jeans. Then I returned to Celine's the same way I had come. The cleanup could await my happy return from Iraq.

CHAPTER 32

Thursday, 6:55 a.m., Tegel Airport, Berlin. Of course I hadn't slept at all. At two o'clock, I'd given up trying to sleep and just started pacing around Celine's place. By three o'clock, I was ready to give up "Project Baghdad" altogether. I knew, however, that it wasn't Baghdad that made me nervous, but my fear of flying. First things first.

At 4:24 a.m., sure that I had packed the wrong things—or forgotten the important ones—I checked my carry-on one last time. I took out the small GPS receiver Michael had given me from his sailboat, probably envisioning Celine and me lost in the Iraqi desert. That would be the first thing they would find as I went through customs in Baghdad, giving them an excuse to arrest me as a spy, there to check coordinates for American smart bombs. I ignored that the same could be said about the map of Iraq, attributing my selective thought process to my aerophobia. Finally, I worried about whether Celine's carry-on bag really met the airline's specifications or whether she'd always gotten by on charm.

At 5:31 a.m., far too early, I headed out to look for my cab in Argentinische Allee, shivering from what I hoped was the morning cold and not from fear. I hadn't asked that the cab pick me up at the door. Either I wanted to spare my neighbors the rattle of a diesel engine at that hour, or I was already training to be a secret agent. The real reason was that I wanted to have at least a short workout before sitting in economy-class comfort all day. The cab driver turned out to be Arab, which I took as a good omen.

By 6:55 a.m., numerous surveillance cameras had recorded my every move at the airport and stored them with time and date stamps for future reference; hypervigilant metal detectors had found the keys to my apartment; and sensitive hands had checked to make sure I really was harmless. But only after I had taken off my shoes.

So far I had done just fine: the Arab taxi driver had not turned out to be a bomb-toting terrorist, Celine's carry-on hadn't caused any trouble, and when I took off my shoes, I exposed socks without holes. I wondered whether my luck would hold up.

It was too soon to worry about how to get into Iraq and what I would do when I got there. Before that, I'd have to survive four takeoffs and landings; trust that the pilots and air-traffic controllers were well trained and alert; put my faith in the proper functioning and stable power supply of radar systems, altimeters, and jet engines; and, finally, hope that swarms of birds would kindly keep out of our flight path. Oh, and one more thing: that the various navies that spotted us in the air would not mistake us for a bomber plane.

"Lufthansa flight sixteen-oh-seven to Frankfurt is now ready for boarding."

The people in the front rows were the first to jockey for their seats. According to most statistics, your chances of surviving a plane crash are best if you're seated in the back rows. Which meant I had to wait until the front-seaters had decided which morning paper they would like and who would get to sit by the window. Standing on the Jetway, I let the crowd pull me forward as I wondered whether this was the very same Airbus that had brought that coffin from Frankfurt a good four weeks before.

The crowd stopped again, and some idiot drove his umbrella into my back. Were umbrellas still allowed on board? I was standing directly in front of the passenger door, by the iron staircase for the crew, when I found myself flooded with second thoughts. Did I really plan to wander through Iraq with Celine's Gucci bag? What, for God's sake, would I do there? How would I find Celine in a country of some 170 thousand square miles? With over 30 million inhabitants, whose language I neither spoke nor understood? By falling back on the useful sentences in my travel guide, which would allow me to order an egg for breakfast and choose between tea and coffee? If Celine was still in Iraq, would she really be in Baghdad? And if she were in Baghdad, she would certainly be in prison. But how would she have written that e-mail and sent it from prison? Wouldn't the Kurdish area north of the thirty-sixth parallel be a more sensible area for my search? Was there any way of getting there from Baghdad? What kind of idiotic plan was this? When the crowd started moving again, I grabbed my bag and raced down the iron stairs.

No alarms, no machine guns. Not even any cries of surprise from the people still waiting to board, who evidently welcomed the prospect of a shorter line. I ended up in the baggage-sorting area under the terminal.

"Where's the person who's been injured?"

The worker looked at me, confused, but clearly trying to understand. I consolidated the surprise effect.

"You people call me away from my patients, make me drop everything, and now you don't even know why you needed me so urgently?"

I held my medical ID under the guy's nose, but how long would he believe that Celine's Gucci bag was a doctor's kit? Especially since an alarm had begun to sound somewhere nearby?

"Listen. You stay right here and wait for the paramedics. Tell them to follow me at once! Got it?"

Impressed with my own coolness and quick thinking, I ran directly toward the sound of the alarm. I was sure it would be most chaotic there, offering me the best chance for escape. I didn't run into anyone in the dimly lit staircase and reentered the terminal unaccosted. The check-in of passengers had been halted, and city and border police were running all over the place, all heading in the direction of Lufthansa flight 1607 to Frankfurt.

Celine's bag turned out to have been a good idea once again.

"Jump on fast. They'll stop all traffic any minute now. We'll be stuck here for hours!"

Deeply grateful to the driver who nervously waved me aboard the public bus back into town, I sank down deeply in my seat in an effort not to expose too much of myself to the world outside my window. The driver seemed to know not only what to expect of nervous airport security, but also that terrorists running around in airports tend to carry hand grenades and submachine guns, not Gucci carry-on bags.

I had left Celine's apartment at 5:24 a.m. Only four hours later, I was back again. I didn't know whether there was a law against not boarding your flight by escaping down an iron staircase. But I knew I had committed one criminal offense for sure: in all the chaos, I had dodged paying the bus fare. In Berlin it's called "subreption of public transport." And if some ticket inspector had caught me, I'm quite certain that he wouldn't have let me count the unpaid fare against my unused plane tickets.

Bundesamt für Verfassungsschutz
Dept. IV, File #286-56

Subject: Dr. Felix Hoffmann
Report #26

Subject has escaped further surveillance. Hoffmann has not been seen for five days, either at his apartment or at South Berlin Hospital, his place of occupation, from which he took a two-week vacation on short notice.

We have come to the conclusion that the subject has learned of our surveillance measures and gone into hiding. To make the best use of limited staff, 24/7 surveillance of his home will be discontinued for the time being and substituted by random site checks.

Bundesamt für Verfassungsschutz
Dept. IV, File #286-56

> Subject: Dr. Felix Hoffmann
>   Report #27

Routine evaluation of video material at Tegel Airport reestablished contact with subject Hoffmann. Further investigation revealed that the subject was connected to an incident there on Feb. 24th: subject had checked in and passed through security for flight Lufthansa 1607 to Frankfurt. Subject then suddenly fled from the Jetway via maneuvering area. Subject had not checked any luggage.

It has been established now that subject had booked a connecting flight from Frankfurt to Cairo (Egypt). Personnel at South Berlin Hospital were not cooperative when interviewed. Yet it could be learned that subject planned a beach holiday at the Red Sea. Present location of subject once again unknown.

Bundesamt für Verfassungsschutz
Dept. IV, File #286-56

Subject: Dr. Felix Hoffmann
From: Department Head
To: Field Force IV

Before reports #26 and #27 are presented to the coordination committee, the following corrections are to be made:

1. Report #26 (lost contact to subject despite 24/7 surveillance) has become obsolete thanks to report #27. Report #26 will be deleted without substitution.

2. Report #27 (evaluation of video material at Tegel Airport) will now be retitled #26.

3. In this report, the term "reestablished contact" will be substituted by the term "identified." The term "routine" is to be deleted. In the last paragraph, the term "once again" is to be deleted.

4. It should be noted in report #26 that the subject undoubtedly had an intimate knowledge of Tegel Airport (layout and organizational details) and probably even personal contacts there. His successful getaway would not have been possible otherwise.

5. In this context, critical understaffing should again be underscored.

6. Regarding interviews at South Berlin Hospital: there are direct flights from Berlin to the Egyptian Red Sea (Sharm el-Sheikh, Hurghada) almost daily; flying via Frankfurt and/or Cairo is most unnecessary. In light of this, the alleged "beach holiday" is most improbable.

7. This office proposes the following explanations for the subject's planned flight to Cairo:

7.1   Planned meeting with subject Celine Bergkamp there (Ref. #286-03)

7.2   Planned meeting with other supporters/terrorists there; e.g., Hamas? Iraqi security?

7.3   Subject wanted to throw us off course.

Conclusion

1. It is beyond a doubt now that the relationship of subject Hoffmann to subject Celine Bergkamp is not only of a private nature, but that Hoffmann is an active supporter of Bergkamp's underground activities, if not an activist himself.

2. Contact with subject Hoffmann has to be reestablished ASAP. 24/7 surveillance of latest known address should be reinstituted, problematic personnel situation notwithstanding.

CHAPTER 33

Had I finally grasped that Michael and Beate were right, that my trip to Baghdad made no sense? Or had my angst about flying simply gained the upper hand?

No. I had awoken from a perpetual state of somnolence as I was about to board the plane. Only then did I realize that, ever since that coffin had arrived at Tegel Airport, I had been living in a state of shock, with only a selective understanding of what was going on around me. Seen from the outside, I had been functioning reasonably well. I hadn't given any absurd orders at the hospital or otherwise put patients in danger. The discreet hints could be considered to be in the realm of normal behavior: wearing my tie inside out at the funeral, arriving at the hospital on Saturday morning after my visit to Celine's parents, no big deal. Such reflections immediately met with the approval of my everready subconscious defense team, which argued that having sex with Beate could also easily be attributed to my impaired state of mind.

"You must understand, Celine, I wasn't in control. I was running on some kind of autopilot!"

That line of reasoning would mean, to be sure, that there could be no occasional relapses with Beate. Which reminded me of Beate's theory that going to Baghdad had been my way of cleansing myself of this sin.

Be that as it may, in the end, I had been right not to go to Baghdad. And not only because of the latest ultimatum from George W. Bush, or because I had no visa, no knowledge of the language, and no clue where to look for Celine.

That she had been able to send an e-mail meant—assuming she really was the one who sent it—that she was probably somewhere in Kurdistan, or always had been in Kurdistan, and was trying to get to Turkey. Searching for her in the alpine world of Kurdistan would have been just as crazy as doing so in Iraq proper. In Iraq, I would have been prey to Saddam's henchmen, while in Kurdistan, I would probably have somehow gotten in the line of fire of one of their bloody clan feuds.

So I was neither scrambling around the Kurdish mountains, stalking the streets of Baghdad, or sunbathing by the Red Sea. However, my apartment remained unoccupied. To be on the safe side, more or less, I had gone back into hiding at Celine's place.

Hiding from who though? Was anybody looking for me?

I knew I could count on my friends Waldeck and Jablonske. I had, after all, booked my flights under my real name, it being quite complicated to do otherwise these days. And although the Verfassungsschutz was a government institution, I imagined that the terms *data collation* and *networking* had by that point made their way even into our security organization. Which meant that the pair would know about my little show at Tegel Airport and would probably be trying to make some sense of it.

"I told you this guy was just playing innocent!" With a proud smile of superiority, constitution defender Waldeck would shove the report and a few pictures across his desk to Jablonske.

"I never said otherwise," Jablonske would retort.

And then they would be on their way—to my empty apartment.
"I told you he would go into hiding!"
"Was there anything you *didn't* know in advance?"
Would they tell their CIA colleagues? Yes, indeed, they would. They would inform the Americans about anything that had to do with planes, airports, and international flights that a booked passenger hadn't boarded.

So I was probably up against our Verfassungsschutz and the CIA, maybe even the FBI, which had been pretty active outside the US lately. Who else might be looking for Dr. Hoffmann?

I was sure I would find out before long. For the time being, though, my position had improved considerably. I was no longer a sitting duck for anybody who wanted to ask me hostile questions or beat the shit out of me over the whereabouts of Sommer's poison-gas-production machine. In fact, that very night I had the opportunity to change from being the hunted to being the hunter. The tables had turned.

Against my better judgment—I should have known better—I searched Celine's kitchen for some kind of food, where I'd hoped to hit upon at least an old can of soup or maybe even a bottle of wine, but to no avail. So after an evening walk to the nearest gas station, I was sitting on her couch about to indulge in a can of ravioli, a chocolate bar, and some Italian wine. What was Celine having for dinner that night? Somehow, I was sure that she was OK and doing fine without me. Knowing her as well as I did, she had surely found help.

Was she still with Heiner? And, if so, was their relationship still limited to their mission? What about our relationship, which was going on five years? What did she expect from me, anyway? Of course, I knew I could find some answers around there. What would stop me reading her letters, searching her laptop? That it just wasn't done? The stern looks from Celine's puppet collection hanging down from the ceiling? Or was it that I was afraid of the answers, afraid of a truth I didn't want to know?

In the end, the only reason I didn't do it might have been that I saw something out of the corner of my eye when I started to attack my ravioli: there was light on in the apartment across the street—my apartment!

Had I forgotten to turn off the lights the day before when I'd gone to pick up those things for my trip? I had not. I'd been there in the middle of the day, when there had been no need to turn the lights on. Besides, as I watched, the lights went on in the bathroom. It seemed that there was an open house again at my place—for the third time in ten days.

I say third time because when I'd been looking for the grenade blueprints the other day to show them to Michael, only to find them in the wrong stack, I was sure there had been a first discreet search. Then, someone had visited both my apartment and my cellar two days before. And here they were, back for search number three, adding to my electrical bill to boot! Whoever was there evidently felt quite at home. Could it be my friends from Verfassungsschutz?

Should I call the police? Even if it were Jablonske and Waldeck or their colleagues, they would still have to do some explaining. But then they, or whoever it was in my apartment right then, would know I must be somewhere nearby. No good. I still made a call, though. After four rings, someone picked up. But no one said anything on the other end of the line; only some breathing could be heard. At least my visitors were curious who might be calling me.

"Tomorrow morning, nine thirty," I whispered in an assumed voice. "The old public pissoir at Chamissoplatz. Be there on time, Felix!"

My visitors left shortly after my call. At least they turned off the lights. Thanks! Hidden behind the curtains, I tried to identify who I'd just invited for a date at Chamissoplatz the next morning.

Two men emerged from the building, but I couldn't recognize them in the dark.

But I did see something else: another truck was parking in front of my place, once again a twenty-four-hour plumbing service. As my two visitors went on their way without particular haste, the back door of the truck opened and a head plus two arms came into view. The arms held a camera with an oversized lens, a low-light amplifier I supposed. Evidently I wasn't the only one interested in who had just visited my place.

I waited a little longer behind the curtain, but saw nothing more. The two men had vanished into the dark, while the truck remained where it was, the back door shut once again. So I took the World War II tunnel back to my place to do some damage analysis.

In order not to further disturb the people from the emergency plumbing service twice in one night, I didn't turn on the lights. But I could tell even in the semidarkness that the earlier guests really had turned my place upside down. My visitors were becoming more brazen every time!

If it had been our Verfassungsschutz, I would have sent the Germany government a stiff bill for cleanup, charging doctors' rates. But, for some reason, I didn't believe that this was the work of the Verfassungsschutz. After all, this kind of chaos was out of character for a German public servant.

CHAPTER 34

Public pissoirs are a European invention, or, to be precise, a French one. They allow for urination in public without the need for an entire building, thus reducing the likelihood of men peeing on buildings, sidewalks, and streets. Found all over Europe in the nineteenth century, most of them have fallen prey to "urban renewal" in the second half of the twentieth century.

The pissoir at Chamissoplatz, one of the last to have survived in Berlin, is well protected these days as a historic monument of sorts. Painted a bold green, the iron pavilion has a roof and is naturally ventilated.

In addition to serving its practical role—enabling what Germans call our "small business"—it had another advantage for my purposes: it stood right out in the open, with no trees or buildings hiding it or its clients from view.

So the next morning, a few minutes past nine, I went to have breakfast in a little coffee shop, where I sat at a window overlooking Chamissoplatz, alone with the waitress, my fair-trade coffee, and organic rolls. The part of Berlin in which I found myself, Kreuzberg, was mostly inhabited by German and Turkish blue-collar workers, who'd already been at work for hours by this time. Increasingly, people who work for Internet start-ups or in fashion were moving in—pushing up rents up so that normal laborers could no longer afford to live there. The new artsy residents considered nine a.m. to be practically the middle of the night. Judging by her pace, I guessed that my waitress subscribed to the latter biorhythm.

With most of the people in the neighborhood either already at work or still in bed, my surveillance job was quite easy. The pissoirs were quite rarely used these days, so I didn't have to inspect a new suspect every minute.

In fact, nobody showed up and nothing happened while I drank my first cup of coffee, neither at the pissoir or anywhere around it. I was sure that the people I had invited to over the phone the night before were watching and waiting, too. And my friends Waldeck and Jablonske? It seemed natural to suspect the people from our Verfassungsschutz of being in that plumber's truck; even the CIA has a standing affair with the plumbing business that goes beyond the notorious "White House Plumbers." But my friends McGilly and Thorne would only be there if they had tapped my phone. Had they, in fact, done just that?

My visitors from the night before had apparently set themselves a time limit, just as I had. At ten o'clock sharp, thirty minutes after the scheduled meeting time, two men showed up and inspected our rendezvous point. They looked Mediterranean, maybe Arabic, Middle Eastern for sure.

First, they walked slowly around the pissoir, which was overdoing it a little. Because the structure stands on iron feet about twenty inches high, you could easily see a person's legs if someone was in there, making inspection of the inside unnecessary. But the pair decided to be thorough and inspected the interior anyway. OK, I supposed I could have been standing on or have drowned in the urinal.

When they came out again, they looked a bit forlorn. The taller of the two men took out his cell phone and placed a call. I could easily imagine the conversation.

"Nobody here, boss."

"Have you checked the place thoroughly?"

"Of course!"

Then the big one looked in my direction. I started to look around the coffee shop for the back door.

"Shall we check the surrounding area, boss?"

"That would be a waste of time! Just come back here."

Of course any number of other conversations were possible, but after putting his phone away, both men ended their mission and started to walk away down Arndtstrasse. I paid my tab and followed them at a leisurely pace. I was on vacation after all.

We walked through half of Kreuzberg, a part of town I'm not very familiar with. But I did recognize the address that the two led me to: 31 Wassertorstrasse. This was where Baran lived, chairman of the United Democrats of Kurdistan, who I had last seen at the fake burial. He was standing on the balcony, talking into his cell phone and waving to his men to come up. Thanks to one of the many trees that make Berlin so wonderful in the spring, he couldn't see me.

From: CIA Headquarters, Langley, Virginia
To: Berlin Station

Unsuccessful detection of the object of interest is not acceptable. Mission remains a top priority. After identifying its location, transport of the object by third party to the country in question is to be encouraged, promoted, and facilitated in every way possible.

CHAPTER 35

Not that I feared I might lose count of them, but I found the
number of people and organizations looking for me or showing
interest in my apartment rather impressive. Had I been voted
Man of the Year and they just forgot to tell me? I already had
on my list our Verfassungsschutz, the CIA, their colleagues on
the Iraqi side—one of whom was probably our efficient visiting
doctor—and Herr Sommer and his crew. It seemed I had to add
Celine's Kurdish friends, the United Democrats of Kurdistan. But
if I wasn't totally off base, this was all about Herr Sommer's damn
water-purification–poison-gas production machine, wasn't it?
What did the Kurds have to do with that? Were they planning
to go into producing poison gas themselves, in order to exact
revenge for Saddam's poison-gas attack in Halabja in 1988?

I was toying with the idea of teaching them all a lesson, and
actually had a plan in mind, but I quickly called myself to order:
this was not the time for games whose outcome was unknown.
Not until I was sure that Celine was safe somewhere, ideally back
here in Berlin.

I didn't have to consider the pros and cons of my plan in any
great detail, because I had received a new e-mail message. Not

directly from Celine, but concerning her—which, in turn, caused me to become concerned.

"Your friend needs your help. Restaurant Behar, Fuggerstrasse. Tonight at nine o'clock."

That sounded like some sort of trap, lacking only the supplementary line "Come alone, no police!" On the other hand, since I was neither at home nor at the hospital, and my cell phone was usually turned off, e-mail was the only way to communicate with me at the moment. And e-mails do sound a little cryptic sometimes. The sender's e-mail address, <u>webmaster@your.service</u> <u>.com</u>, didn't tell me anything. But someone wanted to meet me, and had probably figured out that it was no use to call my cell or try me at my place or at work. Which made me think that it might occur to one of those smarty-pants agents to check Celine's place before long. I realized I should move to a new location soon. But before that, I would accept the invitation to that restaurant. Why pass up a free dinner? And Behar sounded exotic enough; I might discover some new recipe for my collection.

Still, it would be advisable to cover my back. I called Michael at his lab but was informed that "Herr Doctor" was out of town attending some medical convention. So I decided I should at least tell Beate where to look for my corpse in case I never turned up again. I wanted to tell her in person because I knew that she pictured me in some dark dungeon in Baghdad, not stalking pissoirs or my own apartment.

To reach her office at the hospital, I entered via the back entrance. Not only because of the people and organizations on the lookout for me, but mainly to avoid what would certainly happen otherwise:

"Oh, Herr Hoffmann! I know you're officially on vacation, but since you're here now, could you just take a look at…"

The hospital administration occupies the top floor, enjoying plush wall-to-wall carpeting and a magnificent view of

Berlin. I took the stairs, part of my antiaging program. Stepping from the staircase and anticipating the look of astonishment on Beate's face, I had just come around the corner when I saw them: ultrashiny black shoes—four of them, two pairs. Their owners were sitting in the small alcove in front of Beate's office, hidden from view just as I was hidden from them. I knew only two people with shoes that shone like that, neither of whom I wanted to run into. No problem, all I had to do was turn around and walk away; I could return to see Beate a little later. But at that very moment, dear acting department head Professor Kleinweg appeared.

"Oh, Herr Hoffmann! I know you're officially on vacation, but since you're here now, could you just take a look at..."

There was only one option—back down the emergency staircase—and I headed that way. Kleinweg would surely complain to Beate or even higher up about my unorthodox behavior, but I could live with that.

"Dr. Hoffmann! Wait!"

That was said in the southern accent that I associated with Agent McGilly. Or was it Thorne? Either way, I had long since started down the stairs and was at least one floor ahead of them.

It turned into a hasty but almost complete tour of Berlin South. My pursuers had youth and regular training on their side. I countered those with my intimate knowledge of the building, which had seen a number of alterations over the years, making the floor plan somewhat confusing. But still, after some time, regular training began to win out over home-field advantage.

As the distance between us shortened alarmingly, I led my American friends over to the nephrology ward. Orderly Kurt was coming our way, and the two of us go a long way back. Kurt was on his way to the lab, pushing a cart full of twenty-four-hour urine probes in bulbous glass jars that are misused as flower vases in all hospitals.

Kurt didn't greet me; in fact, he didn't acknowledge my presence at all. Strange. I had long since passed him when I heard him call out.

"Watch out!"

A warning that evidently came too late. Although I had easily slipped past his containers of pee, my pursuers had no such luck. There was a loud bang as the cart was knocked over. I heard the sound of glass breaking and fluid splashing—apparently not only onto the floor.

"Damn it!"

"Holy shit!"

In other words, I had the lead again.

But it didn't last long. I was soon wishing that I'd been better about keeping my jogging dates with Michael. The intensive care unit, with its complicated layout, or our operating theaters would have given me an advantage, but that might have interfered with the needs of our patients there. Should I have given up? No, I decided. I still had one last chance at a home-field advantage: the basement. It was a location I knew well, and not only the area where we were storing the equipment for Kurdistan. In fact, everything entering or leaving Berlin South—with the exception of patients and personnel—came through there.

I reached the basement through the cafeteria, astonished as always at how many people were sitting around there long before lunch. From the cafeteria, I took the small staircase leading to the receiving department. Since I didn't run into anyone there, I headed on to the laundry department, which was almost as big as a car wash. Nobody there, either. Could I somehow get agents McGilly and Thorne stuck in the bed wash? That would lock them up for a whole cycle of thorough cleaning. Which may not have been such a bad thing after their run-in with the urine cart!

"Hey, Dr. Hoffmann! We just want to help!"

Right. The friendly assurance had come from much too close for my liking. At that point, I had to make up my mind: go left, to pathology, or right, to central waste disposal and collection? Both directions would take me out of sight for a moment, perhaps long enough to take a decisive turn. In any movie, I would have chosen the hall to the pathology department, giving the director a chance to remind the audience of their mortality. But with my pursuers close behind me, I didn't need to be reminded of that, and the pursuers themselves were probably used to dead bodies. Moreover, this was no movie. Which is why I chose to go in the direction of garbage collection—which proved to be a good decision.

A garbage truck had just finished loading and was turning to leave. I pulled myself up on the little platform in the back where the trash collectors stand during their rounds in the city. That did the trick. By the time my CIA friends rounded the corner, the truck had already left the ramp behind. The ride was a little bumpy, though, so I jumped off at the first red light and disappeared into the nearest subway station.

CHAPTER 36

At least by European standards, Berlin is a big city. To the official population of 3.5 million people, you have to add thousands of tourists, who can be found racing back and forth among the bust of Nefertiti, the Brandenburg Gate, and the few remainders of the Berlin Wall. In addition, two lobbyists and one mistress per parliamentarian, or vice versa, when the German government returned to town. Easily enough people, you would think, to get lost among, at least until darkness falls. Still, I didn't feel safe on the streets or in any of the big department stores. We are used to black people in Berlin, more so with every new genocide in the course of the latest ethnic cleansing in their home countries, but never before had I been aware of how many red-haired men with freckles we have wandering around. I didn't dare to go home or to Celine's place either for that matter. Both my CIA friends and the ones in the plumbing truck must have caught on by then.

Why not hide in a movie theater? It would be dark in there and I'd get entertained to boot. I quickly learned that only theaters with a certain artistic focus are open in the early afternoon. Fine, I might close a gap in my education then!

From what I could discern in the dark theater, it was only sparsely occupied. Still, an odor filled the room that couldn't be ignored no matter how committed the actors on the screen were to their artistic performance.

Suddenly, something nudged my knee. Which was strange, since there was nobody sitting next to me. Was there a dog poking around in there?

"Five marks by hand, ten for the real thing."

I couldn't even make out the gender behind this quietly murmured special offer. I shot up, eager to get out of there. As I was groping my way through the dark, it occurred to me that this friendly service had just been offered to me in good old German marks! A frightening vision came to mind: Was this poor creature that strung out? Or had it been lurking in this filthy theater since before our precious D-marks were changed to euros? Had I passed through one of those notorious wormholes and ended up in a parallel universe, where men had been sitting for years, eyes fixed on the screen and hands under their coats?

Finally, I felt a curtain, behind which was a door, and then a few steps farther a second one, and then a door leading outside. I squinted in the sunshine, but even after I adjusted to the light, I couldn't detect a black- or red-haired man in the crowd. Greatly relieved, I inhaled deeply.

"Helloooo, Dr. Hoffmann!"

Yes, Berlin is a big city, but not so big that I'd escaped incognito. Right when I was trying to inconspicuously make my exit from a porn theater, I had run straight into some giggling nursing students from Berlin South. At that moment, however, even they were preferable to my CIA friends.

An afternoon is infinitely long when there is nothing to do but wait for the evening to come. I tried more than once to get Beate on the phone, but without any luck. The normal movie theaters were open by then, but my lust for the movies had dwindled. I started to ride all over Berlin by subway. The unlit tunnels between the subway stations gave me the illusion that I was somewhat hidden from detection. And as a bonus, I was brought up to date on all the latest street-music hits and the promises of various religions. I heard the same my-name-is-Heinz-and-I-am-HIV-positive story four times; I found other tales of woe on that trip more imaginative.

At eight o'clock, an hour before my dinner date, I left my underground cover at Nollendorfplatz station. The direct route to Restaurant Behar was about three hundred yards. But as I'd learned from mystery novels, I first checked the area by spiraling inward in ever smaller concentric circles toward the restaurant in the center.

Loud music was blaring from inside the Behar, and a sign on the window indicated that a private party was being held there that night, but no especially suspicious-looking types were hanging around the door or nearby. There didn't seem to be anything out of the ordinary going on; in fact, only the *absence* of Turkish- or Arabic-looking men chatting, playing *tavla*, or repairing cars would have been worthy of suspicion in this neighborhood.

Finally, shortly before nine p.m., I reached Beate at home.

"Felix, so you really are here in Berlin! What happened to your Iraq trip? Kleinweg told some wild story about having seen you in the hospital today and how you ran away from him. We were truly worried something was wrong with old Kleinweg. Where in the world are you?"

I briefly explained where I was and why.

"I'm going in there now, Beate. And I'll call you again when I'm done. Let's say, by eleven at the latest."

Then what? What should Beate do if I didn't call her by then? Come swooping into the restaurant with a big roar ninja-style like Superwoman? Call the police?

"But Felix—"

"OK, until eleven at the latest then," I interrupted. I didn't feel all that confident about heading into that restaurant myself; any further reservations from Beate would only have made it worse. I turned my cell phone off again, mustered my self-confidence, and marched straight into the Behar.

Inside the restaurant, the music was even louder. It was astonishing how much noise a few people with small drums, an accordion, a guitar, and a flute could make. Arranged in a big *U* shape, the tables were so heavily laden with food that they looked close to collapse.

A young woman caught my eye. A very young woman, if you subtracted the heavy makeup and all the gold dripping from her. Dressed in a richly embroidered dress over a pair of white pantaloons, her veil held in place by an elaborately braided floral wreath, she was sitting at the head of the *U*, surrounded by men and women in festive clothing. I had been invited to a Kurdish wedding!

The seat beside her was empty, as were a few others. Her future husband and the two families were probably still finalizing the terms of the wedding contract somewhere close-by before he would finally meet his bride in person. For the moment at least, the women held the majority there. I relaxed a bit and studied the food. After all, I hadn't eaten anything all day.

"Dr. Hoffmann?"

A young man dressed in a black suit, white dress shirt, and bow tie had approached.

"Yes, that's me."

"Please follow me."

Which I did. To my disappointment, I was not led to the tables with the food, which would have easily allowed for an extra guest. Instead, the young man led me down a corridor to the back of the restaurant. After passing the bathrooms, we descended a staircase to a big storage room. They hadn't plundered all their reserves for this wedding; two sacks of rice and some giant cans of legumes were stored in there.

I was expected. Not all the men were busy finishing the marriage contract; four had been left to take care of me. How considerate. But somehow I didn't get the impression that they were there to help me get Celine back to Germany. I looked around uncertainly, then tried to break the ice.

"Good evening. Thank you for the invitation."

That was the only thing I would say for some time. The answer to my friendly opening remark, intended to bridge cultural differences, landed directly on my stomach.

From time to time, we do this in medicine, too. It is called preparatory treatment. For instance, we'll wrap a patient in hot blankets to relax the muscular system in order to make a massage more effective. Or, somewhat more aggressively, we'll kill some of the body's cellular defenses with radiation before implanting a new organ. At any rate, preparatory treatment is an effective, proven method. And, if nothing else, it usually saves time.

The men who went to work on me were clearly well aware of it. They believed in beating as a good preparatory method to shorten an interrogation. And they didn't care to waste time seeing me beating as well—beating around the bush, that is. They wanted to get back to the good food upstairs as quickly as possible. I could understand that, though, judging from their blows, they had supplied their bodies with quite enough energy already.

But in the end, my tormentors made a mistake. Again, as in medicine, it is a question of the right dosage, and the four had delivered an overdose. Under the pain of the first five or six blows, I would have told them everything I knew, answered any question to the best of my knowledge. But by the time they finally started to question me, I was already semicomatose. I could still feel the pain they'd inflicted, but had somehow become indifferent to it. It simply didn't hurt so much anymore.

Besides, I couldn't have answered their questions anyway.

"Where is that machine of Herr Sommer's?"

Bang—one more blow to the stomach.

"You're hiding it, Doctor, aren't you?"

Boom—one to the head.

"Or is that pig Baran behind all this?

What could I do? Yell for help? I knew the cellar wasn't sound-proof, since I could still hear music and laughter from upstairs. Of course, they wouldn't have staged all this just for me; they really were celebrating a wedding up there. But I had no chance against the hammering drums and whistling flutes. Besides, even if I had been heard up there, nobody would have come to my aid.

Even worse was that my theory of analgesia by overdose wasn't holding up. I had in no way become indifferent to the pain they'd inflicted. Bullshit. My tormentors had just grown a little tired and began to put less enthusiasm into their blows. Aware of the diminishing effect of their exercise, they opted for a less exhausting—but perhaps more effective—method. From behind the shelves, they produced a car battery and a starter cable. Why couldn't I just lose consciousness? But I was wrong again! Instead, I fell into a deep hole.

"Hey, Doctor, wake up!"

Wake up? Had I only been dreaming? When I tried to move my arm, however, I knew better. I turned my head very slowly to the left, then right. It hurt, but I could do it. My eyelids were heavily swollen, but I could see my surroundings in a somewhat blurred way. I was sitting in the backseat of a car. We were driv-ing under the railroad bridges on Yorckstrasse, heading east. The Irish agent was doing the driving. His African-American col-league, who sat beside him, turned around to look at me.

"Are you awake?"

"Thank you. I am grateful," I stammered.

"No problem."

"Who were those people anyway?"

"Who do you think, Doctor? Comrades of your friend Baran, perhaps?"

OK, so the two had some insight.

"I don't think so. They called Baran a pig. I think they were from the Kurdistan Liberation Soldiers."

Now the Irishman chimed in.

"KLS? What makes you think that?"

"Well, they asked me about Baran, so I have to believe it wasn't his people. And Baran is United Democrats of Kurdistan, UDK."

At least my brain seemed to be functioning all right. I still got those Kurdish groups right.

"So you're working by process of elimination, is that it? Whoever isn't United Democrats of Kurdistan must be Kurdistan Liberation Soldiers. Is that how you see it?"

I nodded in agreement—a grave mistake!

"Stop the car!"

Redhead turned around, saw what was coming, and pulled over to the curb right away. I jumped out just in time. Considering I hadn't had any food all day, it was impressive how much I threw up.

When I was back in the car again, Agent Thorne opened all four windows.

"Where are we going anyway?"

"We're taking you to your hospital, Doctor. At the very least, your head needs to be X-rayed, and I would think you need a few stitches here and there."

Yes, we were on our way to Berlin South, I realized. Not necessarily where I wanted to go. But at the moment, it required all my concentration simply not to move anything, especially not my head.

Redhead turned to me briefly.

"You're not really an expert on Kurdistan, are you?"

I was not in the mood to discuss my knowledge of Kurdistan or, for that matter, anything or anywhere else.

"You think," Agent Thorne continued, "they only have the United Democrats of Kurdistan and the Kurdistan Liberation Soldiers?"

Both agents laughed heartily.

"Doctor, they have at least one party for every valley there, and every one of those groups feels called to fight for a Kurdish nation."

Great. If every one of those organizations planned to interview me on the whereabouts of Herr Sommer's donation—and each of them in their own sweet way—I still had a lot to look forward to.

"How many valleys do they have in Kurdistan?"

We were on Baerwaldstrasse, by then, and I knew we would soon arrive at Berlin South. For a few minutes, it was quiet inside the car, except for the Kurdish folk music still trilling in my head.

"We think you were a guest of the Kurdistan Freedom Army tonight."

I had never heard of them.

"And why do you think that?"

"We've heard that these freedom soldiers launder their drug money at that restaurant."

"So what kind of people are they?"

"Not the good ones, trust me," Redhead answered. "When it works to their advantage, they even cooperate with Saddam Hussein."

"At least that's what their brothers from other Kurdish organizations say," his colleague specified.

I asked them to please drop me off a block away from the hospital. If I was going to go in at all, I was going to take the back entrance again. They stopped when we were still a minute away from Berlin South. As I cautiously started to get out of the car, they gave me some final advice.

"We hope you've learned one thing tonight: You don't have to hide from us. We just want to help. We're the good guys!"

Was that actually the case? Yes, the two of them had saved my butt, no question about that—even after getting that urine all over their shiny shoes in the morning. Then again, how had they known just where to save my butt?

"Don't worry," I told them. "The Kurdistan Freedom Army has limited my radius of operations for the next few days. And when I can finally begin moving again without pain, I'll be back at work at Berlin South, so you'll know where to find me."

Until then, I had a little time left to try to find out what these Americans really wanted from me. And, more important, if they could help get Celine home. Or whether the night just had been a cosmopolitan variation on the "good cop–bad cop" routine to butter up Dr. Hoffmann and convince him to be full of gratitude and trust for the CIA. I waited until I saw the taillights of their car vanish into the night, then I started looking for a cab.

When one finally appeared, I cautiously lowered myself into the seat, still trying to get that Kurdish music out of my head.

Position 08°50´ S / 13°15´ E, Luanda (Angola)
General cargo vessel MS *Virgin of the Sea* has been
sold by its owner, Taiwan Trans Global Shipping
Company, Taiwan. The new owner is the First Middle
East Trading Company, Cyprus. The vessel has been
renamed *Belsazar.* All freight on board is now property of First Middle East Trading Company.

CHAPTER 37

"My God, Felix! What happened? Just look at you!" Judging from the expression on Beate's face, I decided I'd rather not. I tried a faint smile, but even that hurt. Beate quickly pulled me inside and straight to her bathroom.

"Here, sit on the edge of the bathtub."

She pushed the bath mat out of the way with her foot, but too late; a jolly pattern of red drops was already dripping onto it. Still, Beate was focused entirely on me. In the unforgiving light of her bathroom, where I imagined she normally shaved her legs and checked her makeup, I probably looked even worse than I had in the dim light at her front door.

"You want a schnapps?"

That kind of medication, often used in Westerns or thrillers, isn't usually a good idea in real life. I carefully shook my head. Not carefully enough, though.

"I do," Beate said after I vomited, and she ran into her living room.

I gazed after her. It seemed that I had dragged her out of bed, as she was only wearing an oversized men's Canadian lumberjack–type shirt. I inspected myself in the bathroom mirror.

Luckily, it had been dark when I waved the cab down, as the driver would have never stopped for me in daylight. In the morning, he would send me to hell when he discovered the bloodstains on his backseat.

After helping herself to a good gulp of cognac, Beate went to work on me. She carefully drew my shirt over my head and started to clean my wounds with cotton balls and Q-tips from her beauty box.

"Ouch!"

"Keep still!"

"Do you know what you're doing?"

"Don't you worry, mister. I work in a hospital."

After she was done with the cotton balls and Q-tips, she got some disinfectant. She took her work seriously.

"Hey! There are disinfectants that don't burn like hell!"

"Not here. Or are you a private patient?"

Life is unfair. First you're beaten up until, in the truest sense of the word, you're falling apart at the seams, which is not a pleasant experience. Then afterward, the medical treatment isn't much better. Suddenly my personal Florence Nightingale halted her efforts.

"Hey, are you really staring at my cleavage?"

Hard to believe—but yes, I really was, I realized. How close to death do you have to be to not take the opportunity?

"Sorry. It's nothing personal, Beate. It's in the male gene. My genes just don't want to die along with me."

The treatment ended with some bandages. Because Beate's household wasn't prepared for courageous knights like me, one of her T-shirts had to do. After that, she provided me with two aspirin and a cup of peppermint tea.

"You'll sleep here. I'll get the couch ready for you."

Which is how I came to spend my second night at Beate's. Why not combine business with pleasure, my genes suggested,

still worried about their survival. But not only had sleeping with
Beate not been the greatest idea to begin with, but thanks to my
broken ribs and hematomas, two people were safe for the night: I
from my genes, and Beate from me.

I spent most of the next day in bed, or rather, on Beate's
couch, diligently trying to move as little as possible. It would have
been best not to breathe at all, since inhaling was a real terror.
Twice, there was no way around it, and I had to crawl on all fours
to the bathroom. At least that revealed that I had no blood in my
urine, though my kidneys had gotten more than their share the
night before.

That evening, Beate returned with Hartmut from surgery.
After firmly pinching here and squeezing there, he declared that
nothing but a few ribs were broken and that there were no internal injuries.

"Oh man, you were lucky. And the driver didn't stop? It was
a hit-and-run?"

I nodded weakly.

"That'll teach you to stay up to date with your tetanus shots!"

Hartmut understood that I didn't want to become his hospital patient. He didn't know that I was supposed to be on the Red
Sea. So after I presented my bare behind to him for the tetanus
shots, he packed up and left.

"But he'll spread the news around the hospital that I'm loung-
ing around on your couch!"

"No, he won't."

"And why not?"

"Because I asked him not to. I told him that you're officially
not in Berlin. Yes, he thinks that his CEO and internal medicine's
acting department head are having a hot time of it, but he won't
make it public."

I relaxed. I was sure that Hartmut would keep quiet. First,
he wasn't the gossiping type, and second, Beate was his superior.

After Hartmut left, Beate indulged in a long hot bath. When she reappeared, what seemed like hours or days later, in a high-necked bathrobe, she wore no makeup and her wet hair was hidden under a big towel. Her attractiveness didn't rely on makeup or her the elegant way her hair fell, but I wondered once again whether the homely casual dress code represented a certain degree of intimacy between us or whether saw me only as a sexless patient. Or, at most, the friend of her best friend.

Beate had prepared a tray with cheese and wine. I tried some wine, perhaps to wash away the bitter thought of the most likely answer to my unasked question. But the wine led to an instant dizzy spell. It was back to peppermint tea for me.

"So what actually happened to you last night at that restaurant?"

Her bathrobe chastely closed, Beate sat down on the couch beside me.

I told her what I could remember. I still couldn't recall how the CIA agents had rescued me, but I hadn't forgotten my suspicions regarding the very fact that they were there at all.

"Maybe the Kurds and the CIA rigged it in advance. How did the CIA even know where to look for me?"

"From me."

I was surprised.

"The CIA boys?"

"Yes. They'd been waiting to talk to me when they suddenly saw you in the hospital, as you probably suspected. After they'd lost you on that race you gave them through Berlin South, they came back. I wanted to tell you that when you called right before you walked into the restaurant, but you just hung up on me."

Correct. In spite of the later blows to my head, I did remember our phone call. I'd hung up because I thought Beate was going to further diminish the limited amount of courage I had mustered at the time.

"What would you have done in my place, Felix? Of course I didn't trust those CIA guys all that much. Nor did they trust me, I felt. But then I really didn't know that you hadn't gotten on your flight to Baghdad or where you were now. It's not very hard to fake ignorance when you are actually ignorant. I just stuck to my position that I'm only the CEO of Berlin South, and once you go away on vacation, you're none of my business. They finally gave up, but left me their card. You know the magic sentence: 'Call us as soon as you hear from Dr. Hoffmann. He's in Berlin and he's in great danger. But we can help!' Then you called before going into the restaurant. Which was when I realized that they knew much more than I did. And I got increasingly worried the longer I waited for your next call. So, yes, I just called that number on the card they'd given me and told them where you were."

I looked at Beate, still leery of the CIA people.

"When? When did you call them?"

"I told you. I was worried. And the longer I waited for your call, the more worried I got." She was playing with the belt of her bathrobe, wrapping it around her index finger. "OK, I didn't wait until eleven."

Thank God she hadn't. My CIA friends had found me just in time. But it still didn't reveal anything about their motive. Unless there was a new CIA policy to save non-US citizens from being beaten up by other non-US citizens.

I had no idea whether my once-again throbbing head was that the result of heavy thinking or part of a postconcussion syndrome. Either way, I didn't want to think anymore just then. I took two more aspirin, tried to find the least painful position I could manage, and hoped to fall asleep soon.

CHAPTER 38

I spent most of the next day on Beate's couch again, surfing through the world of morning and noon talk shows and soaps hitherto unknown to me. In the afternoon, after a cautious trip to her refrigerator and her bathroom, I prescribed myself a long hot bath. Though it didn't do much for the pain, it relaxed my muscles a bit.

Should I move back to Celine's place? Or even to my apartment? No, I thought, two or three more days of Beate tending to me would do me good. Was that my real reason for staying, though? Or were my genes talking to me again, sniffing around for their just-maybe-after-all chance? In any case, I needed some fresh clothes. In slow motion, I got dressed, then called a cab.

After a five-minute stop at a hardware store, I told the driver to let me out on the corner of Argentinische Allee. I used the old underground path to get to my place. And what a surprise—as far as I could see, I hadn't had any new visitors! The chaos that Baran's people had left me with appeared unchanged. I peeked out the window from behind the curtains and saw that no change there either. This time the side of the truck promised to have my washing machine repaired in an hour or less.

Smirking under my bandages, I unpacked my purchases from the hardware store and began the uncomplicated process of installing automatic timers around the apartment. I set the dials to "random," so that my lights, my radio, and my TV would go on and off intermittently throughout the day. It might not work for long, but I hoped that it might keep those people from the TV, plumbing. and washing-machine services busy for at least a little while—along with their helpful colleagues from abroad.

I packed socks, shirts, and underwear for a few days, and even remembered to throw in a new toothbrush. Then I left my apartment the same way I had come.

Back at Beate's, I saw her car parked in front her building, so I knew she was home from the hospital. Taking each one slowly and carefully, I climbed the stairs up to her apartment. I thought that perhaps I would even tolerate a glass of the champagne I had brought along from my personal inventory. In any event, no more peppermint tea! I rang the bell, and Beate opened the door, smiling all over. She had changed from her CEO suit into a sexy short dress, and she smelled of perfume. I had to remind myself that I was the patient, for whom Beate was doing a favor. But apparently, this was a win-win situation, since Beate seemed equally happy to have me.

"Hi, Felix. Where have you been?"

"I just got myself some fresh clothes. Just in case you want to take me out to a fancy dinner," I answered, pushing Celine's Gucci bag inside with my foot.

At that moment, the door from the bathroom opened, and George Clooney stood in the doorway. Or his younger, even more attractive twin brother. In the sudden silence, my small traveling bag seemed to grow to the dimensions of a trunk.

"Max, this is Felix. Felix, this is Max."

A friendly handshake between Max and Felix. Felix learned that Max was Max Krieger, who owned an advertising agency that

Felix had even heard of. Max seemed to know quite a bit about Felix.

"Good to see that you're on your feet again."

Which—I thought to myself, finishing the sentence for my new friend—means you'll be able to walk away from my turf here. Yes, I clearly had to leave. But then, what would that look like, when I had just hauled my bag in? However, staying at Beate's place and becoming an earwitness to the Beate-Max relationship was not an appealing option.

The situation was resolved when Beate got her coat.

"You'll manage, Felix, won't you?"

A rhetorical question that I answered with a brave smile. I would do my best, of course. But you never knew with postconcussion syndrome. If I had a dizzy spell, I might, for example, fall in the bathroom. I would either die at once from a broken neck, or my head would hit the bathtub, rendering me unconscious, and I would die from hypothermia. But just leave me all alone and helpless, and have yourself a good time!

I stayed at Beate's for two more days, but didn't see much of her, and when I did, it was only briefly. During the day, she was at work, and she spent her evenings with Max. She was a busy woman indeed.

"Everything OK at the hospital?"

"Don't worry, Felix. Even the internal medicine department is running smoothly—though Kleinweg is constantly griping."

Then she grabbed some spare clothes and vanished again.

I was such an idiot! Was it really just male genes? Or was it my never-ending puberty, my crushed male vanity? I remembered the first dinner I'd prepared for Beate, when she had said that "at our age, everybody's in some kind of relationship, more or less." I had to realize that sleeping with me really had been a kind of social mercy on Beate's part. And also that my appeal was getting close to its best-used-by date. It probably was limited to naive nursing students, as long as they didn't see me coming out of a porn theater.

Enough of never-ending puberty and crushed male vanity. Also enough also of playing cloak-and-dagger with underemployed secret agents and freedom fighters. Finally, enough of whatever backroom games might be in play at Vitalis or Berlin South.

The important thing was for Celine to get home safely and to somehow help in that endeavor. I had thought of a plan, but it was one that might put Celine in even greater danger.

So all I could do was check my e-mail five times a day and call my voice mail frequently. Beate had called Celine's parents several times, but they claimed that they hadn't heard from their daughter either.

Had that e-mail with the South Sea shell only been a cruel joke? Or had something become of Celine since her lucky escape?

Bundesamt für Verfassungsschutz
Dept. IV, File #286-56

Subject: Dr. Felix Hoffmann
From: Field Agents
To: Section Chief

Based on our latest observations, we strongly recommend continuing around-the-clock observation of the subject's latest address.
Probably under cover of darkness and/or employing diversionary
tactics, the subject or an accomplice have accessed the subject's
apartment unnoticed and apparently installed timer devices that
activate room lights, TV, and radio at random. Investigation using
directional microphones has not registered any human activity
parallel with the activation or inactivation of the electricity.

The fact that the subject and/or accomplice could access the apartment unnoticed and implement the above-described deceptive
maneuver proves the substantial criminal and conspirative energy
of the subject and/or associates. This makes impending action
(terrorist attack) highly probable.

Bundesamt für Verfassungsschutz
Dept. IV, File #286-56

| Subject: Dr. Felix Hoffmann |
| From: Section Chief |
| To: Field Agents |

Observation of subject's last known address is authorized for one more week (seven days).
[Signature illegible]

CHAPTER 39

And suddenly, a heartbeat later, all was well.

It didn't matter where that damn water-purification–poison-gas machine had disappeared to. Didn't matter what truck disturbed the natural parking order in front of my door that day. Didn't matter what might secretly be brewing at Berlin South. Celine was back! Sure, she didn't look like she'd been away on a spa holiday, but she was alive, relatively healthy-looking, and in one piece.

At first, it seemed that she hadn't changed much, that we'd gotten back the Celine we'd known before. When she wanted to be left alone on her first day back in Berlin, I told myself, sure, she needs her rest, she probably needs a lot of sleep after what she went through. But the following evening, at a big welcome-back party at Beate's, I found her laughter a little too loud and her dancing a little too wild. Later, I found her lying on Beate's bed, which was doubling as a coatrack that night, just staring at the ceiling in the midst of a pile of outerwear.

There were two schools of thought on how to best handle the situation, both of which I agreed with: One group thought it best to leave Celine alone and give her time to readjust to her life here and to us. The other faction held that leaving Celine alone would be a terrible mistake, with potentially grave consequences for her, and that she needed us to be with her more than ever before. The majority of her friends championed the latter option, and everyone suddenly wanted to stage his or her own party for her. That was hardly the way to help Celine readjust, and I decided to take matters into my own hands.

"What would you think about spending a few days in the Spreewald?"

The Spreewald is a biosphere reserve southeast of Berlin comprised of forests, meadows, wetlands, and about a thousand miles of romantic canals linked to the Spree River.

I did not consider myself the ideal psychotherapist and wasn't even sure whether I'd gotten over my perpetual somnolence yet (I had not, I know now). But they say that often just listening to the patient is the bulk of the cure, and I figured that listening to what Celine had to say should be something I could handle without a degree in psychotherapy. The Spreewald would be calm, too, as March isn't exactly high season there. And work wouldn't be an issue either. Though it was hard to believe, my second week of vacation was only just about to begin.

Which is how Celine and I found ourselves the following evening studying the menu at the restaurant of a hotel called Zum grünen Strand der Spree, which means "on the green banks of the Spree." Two years before, I had buried those South Pacific shells for Celine nearby. The *Cytherea meretrix*, whose picture had given us hope that she was alive.

Ever since leaving the autobahn, I had noticed a red Ford behind us, and I'd wondered whether it was following us. Driver and copilot were seated two tables away, apparently still undecided between the chef's recommendation of the day, filet of boar with fresh local cèpes and hash-browned potatoes, and the house specialty, zander with tomatoes and capers on creamed sauerkraut with parsley potatoes. But why should Celine and I be the only ones who had decided to spend a few days at the Spreewald?

"Those two over there, are they staying here, too?" I asked Torsten. Torsten used to be a colleague of mine in the X-ray department of Berlin South, but for several years, he'd been running this hotel and restaurant with his wonderful wife, Anja.

"Yes, they are. They even paid for the first night in advance."

"Did they have a reservation?"

"No, they didn't. They said it was a spontaneous decision."

"Well, maybe they just adore the Spreewald in early spring, when it's still cold and wet here and the storks haven't come back from Africa yet. Just like Celine and me."

"In any case, they've got somebody paying for their spontaneous decision."

"How do you know?"

"They said they'd pay cash if I gave them a bill for double the amount. But I won't do that. I don't go for people living off their business expenses."

"Maybe they just want to cheat the IRS."

"I don't think so. They didn't want separate bills. But whatever."

Celine was in the ladies' room while I was having this hushed conversation with my old colleague. Not wanting Celine to worry, I hadn't pointed out the Ford to her.

Celine seemed to sleep rather deeply that night, though she occasionally tossed around a bit during what I imagined was a bad dream. Then I took her lightly in my arms, telling her everything was all right.

Only the next day did I realize that her problems were not only psychological. I had planned a mountain-bike tour through the Spreewald, but we ended up just walking around a bit.

"When we get back to town, I want you to have a checkup at the hospital first thing. Don't worry. I'll stay out of it completely."

"I'm fine, Felix. I just need a little rest, that's all."

Neither on our drive nor on our walks did she tell me anything about her journey. Whenever I tentatively brought up the subject or got anywhere near it, she just ignored me or played dumb. Meanwhile, on the international level, news from Iraq had given room for some hope in recent days. The Iraqis had begun to dismantle their missiles, the UN weapons inspectors spoke of "Iraqi cooperation," and they still hadn't found any weapons of mass destruction. Would the US and Great Britain really just ignore all this and still go ahead with their plans? But then, that would mean that the people in Iraq would be stuck with their mad dictator. Could we, rightly believing in the universality of human rights, ignore *all that?* Ignore it for the sake of keeping another "peace in our time"?

We spent that evening once again in the silent company of the Ford drivers. Celine didn't order a full dinner for the second night in a row, but at least she had some fresh zander from the Spree River with her salad. After a few bites, though, she gave up.

"I'm sorry, Felix. Don't let me spoil your appetite. I just need a little fresh air."

"Want me to come along?"

"Thank you, but no. I'll be back for dessert."

After Celine left, I asked Torsten if we could have a second bedroom. Perhaps sharing a bed was the problem, or part of it.

"Sure. No big run on this place until April or May."

Celine wasn't back by the time dessert was served. Nor was she in our room. I walked all the streets of the village—all four, to be exact—but there was no trace of her. Had she taken one of our hiking trails and gotten lost? Fallen into one of the romantic canals and been too exhausted to get out by herself?

I returned to the hotel to ask Torsten for a flashlight.

"Wait a minute, Felix. I'm coming with you."

Torsten dug up two flashlights, and we decided that splitting up would be more effective. After a good hour of searching and calling her name, the batteries were dead and we met back up at the hotel.

"What if she just went home to Berlin?"

My car was still sitting in front of the hotel.

"How would she have gotten there? Besides, she would have told me…I think."

Suddenly I knew exactly what had happened. I stormed straight to the hotel bar, where the two Ford types were smirking into their drinks, obviously very pleased with themselves. I had the advantage of surprise on my side, which made it easy to push the smaller of the two off his barstool while I grabbed his comrade by the jacket.

"What have you pigs done to her? Where have you taken her?"

On their own, either one of them would surely have been able to take me on, but by then, Torsten was holding me from behind.

"Felix, cut it out! They've been sitting here all the time."

They just reminded me so much of Jablonske and Waldeck that I was sure they were Verfassungsschutz. But it was true, if they had kidnapped Celine, would they be sitting there just then? Or were those simply diversionary tactics? Who else might have kidnapped Celine? The Iraqis? Hoping to demonstrate that you couldn't get away from them after all? Or one of the Kurdish parties, like the Kurdistan Freedom Army, who had interrogated me so politely the other day? Any number of groups could be responsible.

"Could it be that you're just a bit paranoid, thinking the whole world is after Celine? Maybe she just wants to be left alone, even from you, my friend," Anja suggested.

I finally checked our room for Celine's stuff. Her traveling bag was still by the bed, and her clothes hanging in the wardrobe. But in the bathroom, her electric toothbrush was missing, as was her wallet. I heard Torsten talking on the phone behind me.

"A young woman, you say? Yes, I understand. All the way to Berlin. Thank you very much."

Torsten had called the only cab driver in the village and got his wife on the phone. Her husband was on his way back from Berlin, where he had driven a young woman.

Anja made me a double espresso, and I hit the road. I reached Berlin around three a.m. and found Celine at once: on my answering machine.

It was like Torsten had said. She needed some rest, had a lot to think about, had to find herself, etc. I shouldn't worry, and I shouldn't come looking for her.

So I jumped right back in my car and rang Beate out of bed.

"Celine's not here, Felix."

I didn't believe her.

"May I come in?"

I didn't wait for her answer and simply pushed my way in to check her place. No, Beate was not alone. But it was her friend Max, not Celine, in her bedroom.

"Felix, I have no idea where Celine is. And even if I did, I wouldn't tell you. She needs some time. Alone."

Max then had the nerve to barge in.

"Don't you think you should respect your friend's wish?"

I had already used up most of my energy on the guys at Torsten's bar, and even if I hadn't, it wouldn't have been a good idea to try anything on Max, who looked like he went to the gym regularly. Besides, people get even more annoyed if you just ignore them.

"Beate, did it never occur to you that Celine might still be in danger even here, back in Germany? That she might need help?"

"Felix, spare me your paranoia. We're in Germany, not the wilds of Kurdistan."

Torsten's wife had also mentioned paranoia. But in the medical field, a diagnosis isn't final simply because two doctors are in agreement. Moreover, Beate was ignoring an important point: an ultramodern, ultrapowerful atomizer for the production of poison gas was still hidden somewhere. And experience has shown that people, especially loved ones, are a solid argument when somebody wants to trade them for something he really wants.

Operation Enduring Freedom—Horn of Africa

(OEF-HOA)
From: Frigate *Bayern,* position 17°23' N / 52°19' E, eastern Gulf of Aden
To: Joint Special Operations Command Germany, Geltow

Daily report on shipping activity in surveillance and reconnaissance area (excerpt):

MS *African Star,* oil tanker, from Kuwait to Durban, suspect classification: 0. No inspection.

MS *African Queen,* oil tanker, from Kuwait to Durban, suspect classification: 0. No inspection.

MS *Morning Beauty,* container freighter, from Hamburg to Bandar Abbas, suspect classification: 1, freight documents checked, no irregularities. No inspection.

MS *Belsazar,* General cargo vessel, from Luanda to Karachi, suspect classification: 1, freight documents checked, no irregularities. No inspection.

MS *Exxon Bremen,* oil tanker, from Emden to Dubai, suspect classification: 0. No inspection.

CHAPTER 40

I kept Celine's parents' row house under surveillance for twenty-four hours. After that, I was pretty sure that she wasn't hiding there, so I rang the doorbell. The information I gained yielded nothing new.

"We have no idea where Celine is. And even if we knew, we wouldn't tell you."

I had at least been given breakfast at Beate's. At the Bergkamps', I again wasn't offered so much as a cup of coffee, let alone an invitation to use the shower. The only reason I hadn't frozen to death was that I'd found my sleeping bag among all the junk I carry around in my car.

Considering the relationship between Celine and her parents, I hadn't been very optimistic that end up there. And even if she had chosen her parents' house of all places to "find herself," she wouldn't have let me sit out in the cold for so many freezing hours and not even treat me to a hot drink—I hoped. However, I had come up with a new theory on why she was avoiding me: She knew about me and Beate; Beate had told her. She was punishing me! Still, I was certain that she was in danger and that I should find her before someone else did.

But where else could I look? Was there an old friend from school I didn't know about, or some favorite uncle who was still alive? I was on my way back to Berlin, pretty much at a loss, when it suddenly occurred to me that driving toward Hamburg had perhaps been the right direction after all. I just needed to keep going—toward Enge!

Situated on the Elbe River about sixty miles from the North Sea, the port of Hamburg is pretty far north. But the little village of Enge is even farther north, just a few miles from the Danish border. Celine had once told me that her aunt had a cottage there, which was uninhabited most of the year. We had planned to go several times but hadn't made it yet. For lack of any better alternative, I headed there.

Enge, I discovered two hours later, was extremely small. It consisted of a country store that doubled as a post office, an inn to celebrate weddings and host funeral meals, and a church with services every other Sunday. Not even a war memorial. As I passed the sign announcing that I had entered the village, I realized that even there the era of chickens happily pecking around on the roads was long gone. Some idiot training for the motorcycle speed record cut me off from the left, while a tank-sized combine harvester honked its horn from behind.

I ran into Celine at the store, where I was about to ask for directions to her aunt's house. At first, it looked like she was about to scurry away, but then she evidently changed her mind.

"You can come over for a coffee and a shower. And then I want you to leave."

Half an hour and a nice warm shower later, we were sitting in the kitchen of the cottage, under dried flowers hanging from wooden beams and surrounded by antique pots and pans. Outside, spring was clearly on the way: chicks were preparing their nests in the garden, and a continuous procession of tractors chugged along the country road. Celine was drinking mineral water, while I sipped a local beer I had bought for myself at the country store.

Although it hadn't even been two days since I'd last seen her, she seemed much more relaxed. Her eyes had some of their sparkle back, and her movements were less agitated. In Berlin and the Spreewald, she had avoided my questions about Iraq and Kurdistan. This time she brought it up herself.

We had been in close e-mail and cell-phone contact throughout her trip across Eastern Europe and Turkey, and I remembered the half-amused, half-frustrated messages from the days when she and Heiner had been waiting for permission to enter Iraqi Kurdistan. We'd lost touch when she got to Kurdistan, but Celine said things there had gone rather smoothly, and the people had been hospitable and helpful. Aside from the hazardous routes through the mountains and the Kurdish truck drivers' bizarre interpretation of the rules of the road, reaching their destination of Dahuk had been no problem. There, the Kurds had quickly unloaded their trucks, with the exception of Sommer's water purification plant.

"They said they'd pick that up tomorrow. Then they launched a big celebration in our honor."

"That water purification plant, Celine…" I tried to interject, but she continued with her story.

"Everything that happened after that was pure chance, the wrong place at the wrong time, or the right place, suit yourself. In any event, that first night in Dahuk, Heiner and I were wiped out from all that driving and went to bed while the party was still going on."

I don't think that I so much as blinked, but Celine clarified for me nevertheless.

"They are extremely conservative in Kurdistan, Felix. We each had our own room, of course. At some point early in the morning I woke up, shivering from the cold. It was still pitch-black, but the party was over. I wanted an extra blanket and went to get my sleeping bag from the truck, but once I was in the truck, I just crawled into the sleeping bag there, as I had been doing for weeks. I fell asleep again at once. I was so used to the hammering of the truck's diesel engine and the rumbling of the road by then that I didn't think anything of it at first when I woke up. And then I was only curious where we were going."

"You weren't scared at all?"

"Well, yes, a bit. But what were the alternatives?"

True. I certainly wouldn't have banged on the driver's cab and alerted some stranger to my presence either.

"So there I was, sitting in the back of this truck, and all I could do was wait and see. I didn't realize that we'd crossed the thirty-sixth parallel into Saddam's Iraq, since in that part of the world, you're stopped at some roadblock every few miles. After several hours, we arrived at our destination. The engine was cut, the cargo door was opened, and I found myself looking into the very surprised faces of a bunch of Iraqi soldiers. We were in some factory that didn't seem to have anything to do with water purification. The soldiers were wearing protective overalls, and some of them, gas masks. There were barrels with skulls and crossbones all over the place. Only then did it dawn on me that we hadn't been hauling a water purification plant through Europe, or half of one, but some present for our friend Saddam Hussein!"

I stayed quiet, waiting to see whether Celine would talk about her arrest, the interrogations, the prison conditions, aware that those were the sensitive topics. But she just leaned back and folded her arms behind her head.

"So that's how I got into Iraq-Iraq. Now I'm tired."

While Celine took a shower, I sat down on the steps outside the front door. Considering it was early March, it wasn't too cold. Since the village was only dimly lit—it didn't suffer from light pollution like Berlin—I sat there waiting for the stars to appear. Celine stuck her head out and wished me good night, then disappeared again. I wasn't sure what she meant—was I invited into the house or not? Probably not, I decided, so I walked over to the village pub for a good-night beer.

My sleeping bag's label claimed that it had been tested in the Himalayas. So after a second good-night beer at the pub, I hauled an outdoor lounge chair out of the shed, grabbed my sleeping bag from the car, crawled into it, and waited for the March snowstorm that I had no doubt would descend upon the area that night. While waiting, I thought about Celine and what was wrong with her. Why was she still so withdrawn? Had she been tortured in Iraq? Raped? And why had I so utterly failed in my efforts to help her? Would she ever laugh at my hilarious jokes again?

I woke up in the middle of a dream that I was taking a shower. Fat North German raindrops were falling onto my face. When turning neither to the left nor right stopped the downpour, I grabbed my sleeping bag and hustled over to my car, where I wished that I had a camper—or shorter legs.

The morning got off to a promising start. It was still raining, but I had coffee brought to my bed, or rather, to my car. Celine seemed to be in good spirits. Dressed in oilskins, the national uniform in Northern Germany, we walked to the store to get some fresh rolls. I was informed that the last bakery in the village had closed down three years earlier. So the locals instead got factory-made rolls—made by a company that called itself The Country Bakery.

Still, once I had showered, the gorgeous smell of fresh rolls and freshly brewed coffee filled the cottage, nicely counterbalancing the weather outside.

"Where did you get this awesome marmalade?"

Marmalade wasn't quite the right word for this spread, which, as far as I could tell, was made from plums and oranges, seasoned with a whiff of ginger mint.

"Uwe Lorenzen's store in Leck, the next town over. You wouldn't believe that place. In a space not much bigger than this cottage, you can get anything you could ever want; in Berlin you'd have to go to the vast food halls in one of the department stores to find this kind of selection."

So we chatted over breakfast about Uwe Lorenzen's store in Leck and Northern Germany's food specialties. We probably even discussed the weather. I eagerly avoided bringing up Iraq, Celine's friend Heiner, and, for similar reasons, Beate. Until Celine asked why I hadn't come in the previous night.

"At least when it started to rain. The door wasn't locked, you know."

"I didn't want to frighten you, or wake you up. Besides, you might have misunderstood."

"Misunderstood? Misunderstood what?"

I coughed slightly. "Well, I mean, you surely wouldn't have walked out on me in the Spreewald if Beate hadn't told you… what happened between us."

Celine looked up from her coffee and I realized at once that I had just blundered into dangerous territory. It seemed I was the one to break the happy news to her. But the problem went beyond that.

"You really think it was all about you when I fled from the Spreewald, don't you? About the fact that you and Beate had it off with each other while I enjoyed my fantastic vacation in Iraq? Oh, Felix! Can you, just for a minute, try to realize that you're not the center of the universe?"

That must be a pretty desolate universe! Believe it or not, I did not say that out loud. I forced myself to try not to save the situation with one of my famous humorous remarks. For a change, even my monstrous ego realized that life on this planet could possibly exist without me or the question of what Beate and I had done with each other. That I had just vandalized any trust that I had carefully worked to rebuild with Celine again over the last twenty-four hours. And that there was no repair or cleanup crew in sight.

I didn't leave Enge at once—or rather, I wasn't dismissed at once. For strictly practical reasons. Celine had promised her aunt that she would prune the fruit trees, but auntie's antique wooden ladder was far too heavy for her to carry alone.

"Are you sure March is the right month to prune these trees?"

"No idea. But I promised my aunt. Here's a saw for you."

We both ignored the advice you get in couples counseling to "talk it out" and attacked the knotted trees in silence. Although you might not solve your relationship problems this way, at least you don't make things worse, which is entirely possible to do when "talking it out." By the time we were done, the trees didn't look as though they would ever attract birds or bees again, let alone bear fruit. But Celine decided that I had earned myself a good helping of ham and eggs. Which was good, because I had some questions that I thought were safe to ask despite the situation.

"Incidentally, have you spoken to Baran since you got back?"

"No, I haven't. On the one hand, I simply can't imagine that he's got anything to do with that extra cargo. On the other, I'm afraid to ask."

I told Celine how Michael and I had discovered what the supposed water purification machine really was and how it had suddenly disappeared. Then I explained how Baran's people had broken into my apartment, how I'd invited them to that old public pissoir at Chamissoplatz and how they'd led me straight to dear Baran.

"I agree that's strange and raises questions. But it doesn't prove that Baran and his people are behind it."

I had to agree. But that only made it all the more urgent that we find the missing link between Herr Sommer and his customer, Saddam Hussein. I explained my plan to her, the broad outline of it at least. Since Celine was back in Germany, my plan no longer put her in danger. And it was the sort of scheme that I thought would be exactly Celine's cup of tea—the Celine I had known from before, at least.

When I had finished describing it, however, this Celine merely asked, with little enthusiasm, "And you think it'll work?"

I had no idea—but I didn't have any better idea, either.

The rain had stopped by then. With any luck, I could be back in Berlin by evening. Celine said she planned to stay at the cottage for another few days.

"At least lock the door and check that the windows are closed before you go to bed. For all we know, you're the single outsider who witnessed what they unloaded from your truck in Iraq."

Celine promised that she would. When I was about to go, she came to the car window.

"By the way, Felix. Did you know that Beate's pregnant?"

Bundesamt für Verfassungsschutz
Dept. IV, File #286-56 and #286-03
Subjects: Celine Bergkamp, Felix Hoffmann, MD

Field Report:
Through a maneuver apparently planned well in advance, subjects evaded further surveillance at Schlepzig (Spreewald). Subject H. was significantly involved in the diversion maneuver. The subjects' present location has not yet been determined.

Further investigations of subject H. have established how subject came into possession of material found in his apartment following an anonymous tip to this department (including blueprints for the construction of chemical and biological bombs): this material was given to the subject as part of an antiterrorism exercise arranged jointly by the department of interior and department of health. So far, there is no evidence that the subject has made use of this material.

Although suspicious evidence against subject H. has diminished somewhat, the possibility that he will or has passed material on to a third party cannot be excluded. That subject took part in this exercise only to gain access to said material (and to get an overview of planned countermeasures against international terrorism) also remains a possibility.

The motivation for subject H.'s actions remains unclear but suspicious. This refers primarily to:
- his involvement in the above-described incident in Schlepzig (Spreewald), where he and subject B. evaded surveillance.
- the fact that the owner of the hotel and restaurant in Schlepzig (Spreewald), is a former colleague of suspect. Now collaborator?

- the fact that this former colleague was an X-ray and radiation specialist at Berlin South Hospital, workplace of suspect H. Intimate knowledge of problems and procedures in the realm of radiation must be assumed!
- the question of why the subject took vacation from work on short notice in the first place.
- his not boarding a flight to Cairo via Frankfurt but instead fleeing from the airport, probably with the help of a third party.
- the installation of timers in his apartment.

It has been established how subject gained access to his apartment without being detected: buildings in this area are all connected by tunnels, stemming from safety measures implemented during WWII. It must be assumed that suspect became aware of surveillance measures and evaded surveillance by using these tunnels.

Although the case against subject H. has diminished somewhat—specifically with respect to the documentation found in his apartment—observation of subject and/or his last known address in our opinion still has priority in view of his repeated efforts to evade observation.

Expense report from hotel and restaurant Schlepzig, Spreewald:

Because of the above reported evasive actions of the subjects, field officers could not wait for a printout of the bill. This is why expenses are listed without documentation. The high total of expenses is due to the exclusivity of the location, use of which was necessary in order to keep close contact with subjects. We recommend countersignature of the expense account by department head. We do not recommend approaching the hotel and restaurant for post hoc billing, which could lead to unwanted attention in ongoing investigation (again: owner of hotel and restaurant is a former colleague of suspect!)

Handwritten note:

a) 24/7 surveillance of subject Hoffmann is to be discontinued (staff shortage), but investigation is to be continued. Find that lady!!

b) expense report: passed on to accounting

CHAPTER 41

Enge–Flensburg, country road, 280 miles from Berlin: Congratulations, Felix Hoffmann, MD! Ever heard of safe sex?

Flensburg–Schleswig, autobahn, 260 miles from Berlin: Wait a minute. What about George Clooney with his advertising agency? Didn't he have a few more chances than I did to achieve paternity?

Schleswig–Rendsburg, autobahn, 240 miles from Berlin: Actually, what about timing? Wasn't this a little early to be sure about pregnancy?

About midway between Enge and Hamburg, the autobahn crosses the Kiel Canal, which links the North Sea to the Baltic Sea. People stop there to admire the cruise liners and freight ships passing through the meadows dotted with happy cows and canola fields. That's where I stopped to call Beate.

"I'm pregnant? Not that I know of—and don't you think I would be first to know? Who said so? Celine?"

I was greatly relieved. Not only about my nonfatherhood. But more so over the fact that Celine, in spite of everything she had been through recently, was displaying normal human reactions.

"When are you going to show up back at work, Felix?"

"I'm still officially on vacation this week. If nothing new crops up with Celine, I should be back on Monday, right on schedule."

"Take your time. There's a little surprise waiting for you here that you won't really like. And it's not that I'm pregnant."

That sounded like bad news. But since Beate didn't sound particularly worried—mischievously amused, in fact—it seemed that it was bad news for me specifically rather than the hospital. I didn't inquire any further, as I would know soon enough.

First I had to get back to Berlin, where I planned to find out who had cooperated with my good friend Herr Sommer on misusing Celine and helping old Saddam produce weapons of mass destruction.

My old plan had been a simple trade-off: Celine's safe return in exchange for the second part of the "water purification machine." Initially, that plan had only one significant flaw: that I myself didn't know the machine's whereabouts. It actually had two flaws, because Celine was no longer lost in Iraq, but rather, sitting beneath heavily pruned apple trees in Enge, Northern Germany—while that apparatus remained lost. But then, plan A was still the only plan I had.

I persuaded myself that it could still work. After all, as I had learned, rather painfully at times, several parties were sure that I knew where that machine was hiding. In fact, the only person who knew that I didn't was the person who had stolen the thing. And only Celine's friends—and probably our Verfassungsschutz— were aware that Celine was back in Germany.

As I drove south, I made a mental list of all the people to whom I should extend my special offer. The Kurds around Baran who had helped get the first transport under way. The Kurds who had beaten me up at their restaurant. The Iraqi chargé d'affaires who had so warmly invited me to visit his country. The pair from the CIA who had perhaps saved my ass. And, although their interest in the machine seemed limited, I thought it only fair to include my friends from the Verfassungsschutz. I did not put Herr Sommer on my list, as his involvement in the case seemed clear enough.

That evening, back in Berlin, I took the Iraqi embassy off my list. I would make my offer to them via our guest doctor Hassan. I got ahold of him at the hospital.

"Herr Hoffmann! What a nice surprise! Are you calling from Egypt?"

Right. If I wanted to put my plan into action, I should also officially return to Berlin.

"No, I'm back in Berlin."

"That's good. Have you heard from your friend?"

"No, I'm sorry to say. Any news on her from your family or friends at home?"

"I understand my uncle might be onto something, but he's still waiting for more information. I'm afraid I don't have anything concrete for you yet."

His uncle? Hadn't it been his brother-in-law the last time?

"Thank you, anyway. Actually, I have an idea that might work. The thing is, I have something that I gather some people would really like to have. So what I'm going to do is have an auction for it tomorrow in Treptow. On Kiefholzstrasse, at the corner of Elsenstrasse."

Was it thanks to his good manners that Dr. Hassan didn't ask what I was talking about, or did his not asking me make him even worthier of suspicion? All he did was wish me good luck and inquire when I'd be back at work. Probably Monday, I told him.

"Next Monday? The same day as our new department head?"

So the bosses at Vitalis had appointed a new department head. That must be the surprise Beate had mentioned. But I couldn't admit to our guest doctor that I hadn't yet been informed properly.

"Yes. See you then."

I immediately tried to get Beate on the phone. No luck. OK then, back to plan A. But I waited until the next morning before calling the other people I wanted to invite to my trade-off bazaar.

Celine had given me Baran's telephone number before leaving for Kurdistan, and I left my invitation for the Kurdistan Freedom Army with their favorite restaurant, the Behar. After that, I called the US embassy.

"Guten Tag, this is Dr. Hoffmann speaking. I would like to talk to your Mr. McGilly or your Mr. Thorne."

"One moment, please."

After what turned out to be a pretty long moment, I was informed that neither a Mr. McGilly nor a Mr. Thorne was known at the US embassy in Berlin.

I tried a shoddy trick.

"Fine. Just give me the department where they're not employed."

"And which department would that be, sir?"

So much for clever tricks. I had to rely on my relevant book knowledge again.

"The cultural affairs department, please."

The cultural affairs department seemed baffled. Did these people really only track down good seats at the opera for visiting businesspeople from the Midwest or reserve rooms in youth hostels for string quartets from Cincinnati? Should I have asked the switchboard to just put me through to the CIA resident agent? I got a little impatient.

"No, I don't want to talk to your trade people. And no, you got that wrong. I don't want to sell a water purification plant, either to the US or to Iraq. Just be kind enough to take down a short message: Dr. Hoffmann is offering the missing part of said water purification plant in exchange for the safe return of Ms. Celine Bergkamp from Iraq. Tomorrow, at noon. At Kiefholzstrasse, corner of Elsenstrasse. Have you got that?"

The girl said, yes, she did, but she didn't know what to do with the note.

"Listen. If I really am speaking to the wrong department, just hand my message to your security people. Thank you very much."

Security people! That, I thought, was a clever term to use. Why hadn't I thought of it before? But I was still pretty proud of myself.

CHAPTER 42

Berlin, urban district of Treptow, Kiefholzstrasse, corner of Elsenstrasse: This address had terrorized me for years. That was back when Treptow had been part of East Berlin and East Berlin the capital of the German Democratic Republic. Always short on something, be it raw materials, exotic fruits, or spare parts for their cars, the people of the German Democratic Republic had constantly been preached three things by their one-party government: that they were the better Germans, that one day they would surpass the industrial production and the standard of living of West Germany, and that some of their products would soon reach—or indeed already had reached—Western quality. The term they actually used was *world-class*. But how would the people in the Democratic Republic have had any way of finding out whether they'd reached world-class yet? The party had built a wall around their seventeen million devoted followers to keep them sequestered in their socialist paradise. There was, however, one exception: people in retirement were, after wading through tons of bureaucracy, allowed to visit their relatives in the West once a year—and hopefully wouldn't return, thereby relieving the state of its obligations to them during their retirement. That's how my grandmother crossed from East Berlin to West Berlin every year at Christmas, bringing with her wonderful chocolate from this chocolate factory on Kiefholzstrasse, at the corner of Elsenstrasse. The stuff, apparently produced from some ersatz material, or rejected by their socialist friends in Cuba, tasted downright awful but had to be eaten and enjoyed in order not to hurt my grandmother's feelings. In my opinion, this factory should have been the first to be liquidated after German reunification.

For almost fifteen years, the building had just sat there, most of its windows and doors vandalized, mostly likely waiting to be torn down and replaced by yet another fashion outlet mall. It was time, however, for the old factory building to be put to use again. It was where I had invited the various parties for my auction.

Being a responsible host, I was a good hour early so that I could observe who had accepted my invitation. Which was as far as I had gotten with plan A. From that point on, I would be playing it by ear. It was like an experiment from the early days of hard science: you throw some chemicals into a pot and wait to see what happens.

I eased myself into a half-broken chair in one of the hasbeen offices located in the former administration section of the building and looked through the broken windows. Although I had shown up early, others had arrived even earlier. I spotted a plumbing truck at the end of the street. But I knew there wasn't any business for them there and, moreover, the very same truck had repeatedly blocked the parking space in front of my door.

Only minutes later, their colleagues from across the Atlantic arrived, true to their corporate identity in a black Ford. They didn't get out of their car either, and just sat there, enjoying the scenery. Being experienced field agents, they had probably brought some fast food along.

So we all waited. A certain nausea slowly came over me, due in part to my growing uneasiness, but also because, even after all these years, the smell of socialist chocolate made from third-rate ingredients was still being emitted by the stones. Nothing happened. Where were the Iraqis? Where were Baran's people and the Kurds from that restaurant? Had ignorant me chosen some Kurdish-Iraqi feast day for this party?

But I was wrong! As I leaned out of the broken window for a better view—and to get away from that smell—my arms were suddenly pulled behind my back and secured in a vise. At least that's what it felt like. Then I was given a friendly push even farther out the window.

"Can we do business now, Doctor?"

I recognized the voice. I had first heard that impeccable German spoken in a harsh accent at—or rather beneath—that Kurdish wedding reception.

"There won't be any business if you push me another inch."

It quieted my nerves somewhat to see that these people seemed open to logical argumentation and agreed that you couldn't do business with a man who had been thrown onto the street from the third floor. They pulled me back into the room a little, without loosening their viselike grip.

"OK, Doctor. Where are you hiding it?"

"I'll tell you as soon you've told me where my friend Celine is and how I can get her back in one piece."

My ultimatum was followed by a lengthy discussion in a language I couldn't identify. Kurdish, I guessed.

"OK, Doctor. We accept your conditions."

Fine. I had offered them something I didn't have, so I suppose it was only fair that they would do the same to me. A classic deadlock. But not quite. First, because my freedom of movement was significantly limited at the moment, but theirs was not; second, it was me against at least four of them; and third, they were armed. In their eyes, these facts probably made up for the fact that they, I hoped, had no idea about Celine's whereabouts.

"So—where is my girlfriend?"

"Come with us!"

They didn't say "please," but that was OK since I didn't have a choice anyway. I was dragged from the office through the old production halls. The sour smell of rotten chocolate intensified, as did my nausea. I hoped they wouldn't punch me in the stomach again. They didn't right then. I gathered that these people didn't care much for the smell in there either, because they sped up, heading out of production into logistics, and then we were back out on Kiefholzstrasse. Nice—but the CIA and Verfassungsschutz were parked on Elsenstrasse! What would become of my scientific experiment? And of me?

But I had underestimated the CIA boys. Just as the Freedom Army people were about to stuff me into their car, Agent Thorne came racing around the corner.

"Freeze, people! Stay put!"

It was probably an issue in many volatile international situations, but my friends from Kurdistan evidently didn't speak much English. At least they neither froze, nor stopped what they were doing. On the contrary. The guy who was holding me so tightly suddenly managed to do it one-handed; with his free hand, he fired a shot at Agent Thorne, who went down in an instant.

I was still not completely jammed into the car when Agent McGilly appeared, tires screeching, behind the wheel of the Ford. He had to decide whether to help his colleague, who lay on the street bleeding, or Dr. Hoffmann, who was being kidnapped and had recently almost puked all over the Ford. Unfortunately, it was all too clear what he would choose to do. I got a last kick, the doors were securely shut, thanks to the law requiring child safety locks in every car, and we were off.

What made things worse was the bad vibe on board. Although I didn't understand Kurdish, I had a pretty good idea what they were talking about.

"Idiot! Why did you have to shoot at the American?"

"Damn Americans! They always betray us! They've sold us to the Iraqis more than once!"

Or something along those lines. Although the driver was aware that they had, for the time being, gotten the CIA out of the way, he soon realized that we were being followed by the twenty-four-hour plumbing truck.

"Who else have you invited here, Doctor?"

Good question. Your brethren from Baran's United Democrats of Kurdistan. And the good people from the Iraqi embassy. For that was what my kidnappers didn't understand: I was much less interested in who would show up at the chocolate factory than who would *not*. Because one thing was clear to me: Whoever didn't show up for my auction probably had a very good reason for not being there. Knowing that the whole thing was a hoax— that I couldn't deliver what I'd offered—because he was the one who had stolen the atomizer in the first place. So who was it? Baran or the Iraqis?

"Nobody else," I lied.

Was that especially clever? Or should I have answered using the well-known "And if I don't contact them within the next thirty minutes, I wouldn't like to be in your shoes"? A superfluous thought actually, since the Verfassungsschutz was still following us!

At that moment, we took a sharp turn, this time down the ramp leading into an old parking garage on Meinekestrasse. I imagined that we'd jump in a getaway car that was awaiting us there, that this stop was all part of an elaborate plan. But we didn't stop and there was no hectic change of cars. Instead, I heard the loud screeching of brakes behind us. The Verfassungsschutz people in their truck had apparently seen the warning "Attention: maximum overhead clearance 7.2 feet" just in time. Which was advantage number one for the Freedom Army people.

Advantage number two was the fact that the ramp going down from Meinekestrasse was only the way in; the exit was all the way around the block on Joachimstaler Strasse. These two facts considerably improved the mood in the vehicle. Not mine, though, as I had just lost my last guardian angels.

Our final destination turned out to be some courtyard, and I recognized where we were: the restaurant Behar. Not a place that brought back that fondest memories! Not only did my skull and stomach instantly recall the location, but this time I was really, really frightened. All the more so because we entered through the back door. All the trouble I had gone to learn to lace my shoes by myself and wipe my butt—had it all been for naught?

We passed through the kitchen, which was already buzzing with activity. A cook was vigorously stirring some sort of soup, as two veiled women cleaned carrots and peeled a heaping pile of onions. Every detail imprinted itself on my mind, but neither the cook nor the two women would remember ever having seen me there, I was sure.

"Another wedding party today? Where's the bride?"

My answer came in the form of another kick in the ass, which helped me down the stairs to the storage room I remembered so well.

"Know what, wisecracker? You might soon be laughing on the other side of your face. I don't think that your CIA friends are going to come to your rescue today!"

Yes, my kidnappers had seen to that.

It was clear what the freedom fighters wanted from me— the same thing as last time. And again, just as before, I couldn't deliver, even if I'd wanted, because I had still no idea where that damn machine was. But there was one important little difference from before: this time, I had claimed that I could indeed deliver! I could see that we were about to have a rather interesting discussion—albeit a rather one-sided one.

"So where is my girlfriend?" I said, trying to keep a poker face and not show how scared I felt. After all, we were all reasonable people, weren't we? Perhaps I could buy some time by sticking to my story a little longer.

The tactic worked, winning me a few precious pain-free minutes. One of those playground-style discussions began.

"First you show us the machine!"

"No, not before you tell me where Celine is and how I can get her back!"

"No, first the machine!"

"No, Celine first!"

Sadly, my negotiating partners soon lost interest in this sort of diplomacy and fell back on their old line of arguing. They no longer even pretend to know anything about Celine's whereabouts. Did that present a chance for me? It was worth a try.

"See? That's precisely as much as I know about where your damn machine is!"

Regrettably, I couldn't even take pride in the fact that they deemed me too trustworthy to have lied to them. So the dance went on. I was proven wrong when I thought the other night that I had gotten to know the full repertoire of their memory-jogging measures. They had some surprising variations in store for me with their fists and that freshly charged car battery. This time, though, it took me a lot longer to finally pass out.

At least I got some reward for all the pain: a wonderful dream during my blackout. As in *Fidelio*, the only opera good old Ludwig van Beethoven ever wrote, in which the incarcerated Floristan has a vision of his wife, Leonore, coming to him angel-like and rescuing him from his tormentor, I dreamed that Celine had come to rescue me. No, I realized, this was no dream. Unlike me, the Kurdistan Freedom Army activists had actually kept their word: they'd freed Celine and brought her there! Bullshit, my one still-intact neuron told me, that can't be, Celine was free and safe already. I could even still hear her diffident "And you think this is going to work?" when I'd explained my fantastic plan to her at her aunt's cottage.

Then I suddenly became certain. It was no dream, at least not anymore. Because the Kurds were using their CIA-proven water-boarding technique on me. I began to cough like mad, desperately trying to remove the water from my airways. It helped a little to breathe through my nose. How strange!

"Hey, Felix, wake up!"

Strange again. Why was Celine, of all people, trying to drown me? I hadn't realized that she was *that* angry at me!

I was hit once again by a wave of water from a bucket Celine held in her hands. She was apparently trying the classic method of resurrection. I had always wondered if that technique only worked in the movies or in real life, too.

Behind Celine I recognized Baran and his people, most of whom I knew from the fake funeral, and two from the public pissoir at Chamissoplatz.

Baran's United Democrats angrily faced the Kurdistan Freedom Army. For the moment, I was not the center of attention—a fact that even my overinflated ego could live with at this particular moment.

After another bucket of water, I came back to my senses, but I still didn't understand what was happening.

"Celine!" I didn't have to point out how happy I was to see her. "Do you know what's going on here?"

"Your exchange plan—hostage for apparatus. We're trading in that machine from Sommer, like you promised. One little change in plans, though. I'm not the trade-in. You are!"

So that question was answered, too. Of the two groups that hadn't accepted my invitation to the old chocolate factory, Baran's group and the Iraqis, it was the United Democrats of Kurdistan who had stolen that poison-gas machine from the basement at

Berlin South. Which explained why I was no longer of any interest. Even the Kurdistan Freedom Army people were finally convinced that I was the wrong person to ask.

"You promised you'd stay in Enge until I sorted things out!"

"And you believed me?"

The situation was absurd: while the Kurds were yelling at each
other, fists in the air, I was bombarding Celine with questions.

"So Baran and his people are collaborating with the Iraqis?
They slipped the first poison-gas atomizer into your transport?"

"No, we're not," Baran intervened in German, pointing at my
kidnappers. "That was our dear countrymen!"

The Freedom Army people couldn't let that go unchallenged.

"We were told it was parts for the oil industry that were on
the embargo list. No harm in transporting them. Who said they
have anything to do with poison gas?"

"I do," I said. "Believe me, I even saw the blueprints."

That quieted the Freedom Army people for a while. Although
they had beaten me up using every trick in the book just a few
minutes earlier, I was apparently considered a trustworthy third
party in this matter. A moment later, however, the accusations
and counteraccusations started all over again, with even more
vigor that before. The two Kurdish groups started arguing in
German. Did they want Celine or me to referee?

This much at least became clear: Baran's people had heard
that the Iraqis had told the Kurdistan Freedom Army to get the
second part of the machine to Iraq ASAP. That's when the United
Democrats of Kurdistan had decided they'd better get that thing
out of our basement fast. Which they'd done.

"We had to act quickly," Baran said, addressing me directly.
"We'd heard by then that Celine's shipment wasn't clean. Plus, one
of my men saw you, Dr. Hoffmann, dining with Herr Sommer, a
known supporter and supplier of Saddam Hussein, at the restaurant Trenta Sei. That's why we searched your apartment."

Yes, I remembered. The flower peddler who hadn't been Pakistani!

Now Baran addressed his countrymen again.

"Doing business with the Iraqis is selling out the interests of the Kurdish nation."

"You too have done business with them. Even the Americans do it!"

This is how it went on, I guessed—the Kurds began butting heads in Kurdish again. A good opportunity, Celine and I found, to slip out without any heartfelt good-byes.

Soon we were sitting in a cab, and with every click of the taximeter, the distance increase from the Kurds—in my case, from the Freedom Army in particular. I remembered that I had not only outlined the general concept of my plan to Celine at her aunt's cottage, but also mentioned the chocolate factory. But that still didn't explain what had saved me at the restaurant.

"How did you know about the Behar restaurant? Did you follow us?"

Far from it. I'd had a pretty good view from that former office in the factory and would have spotted Celine and Baran with his people if they'd been lurking there. And if not there, at least when we were driving through that parking garage on Meinekestrasse. So—how had Celine found me? She gently squeezed my hand.

"Can't you just be happy that we saved your butt?"

Of course I was. So I let the subject drop.

I only learned a few days later what had saved me, perhaps even my life: Celine's proverbial loafing and the fact that she was hardly ever on time. And that my calculation had been wrong, that whoever had the machine wouldn't show up for the meeting. Because although he already had the atomizer, Celine had talked Baran into taking part in my party at the factory, or observing it at any rate. By the time they'd arrived there, however, the party was over and they didn't even get to join in the festive shoot-out. They only ran into Agent McGilly, who was bandaging up his colleague instead of helping kidnapped Hoffmann. But Agent McGilly told them who'd kidnapped Hoffmann. From that point on, it was easy, since Baran knew perfectly well where the Freedom Army's headquarters were—and where they grilled their catch of the day—in every sense of the term.

From:	Office of Special Operations, the Pentagon
To:	National Security Advisory Board, the White House
Ref:	Operation SMOKING GUN

Object Sommer has been located again. It is now in the hands of the Kurdish exile organization Kurdistan Freedom Army. Preparations for its transport to its final destination of interest are being finalized at this very moment.

Relevant parties will be discreetly alerted of its arrival when it has reached its intended destination. Discovery of Object Sommer and immediate publication of the finding can be expected shortly thereafter.

Preparations for the consequences of this discovery and its disclosure should be vigorously continued.

From:	Department of Defense, Baghdad
To:	Bureau of the President
Ref:	Special Shipment #34

General cargo vessel MS *Belsazar* (formerly MS *Virgin of the Sea*) has arrived in Umm Qasr Harbor. Special shipment #34 to the factory at Al Qa'im should now be considered complete. Assembly of production line at Al Qa'im is urgently under way, and the final product will soon be available for implementation.

Diversion via Plan "Exiled Kurds in Berlin" was also successful. It is safe to assume that this plan greatly contributed to the undetected journey of MS *Belsazar/Virgin of the Sea.*

Our officers were commended as instructed, for following orders not to inhibit the escape of German national Celine Bergkamp and for discreetly aiding her safe passage to Turkey. It is expected that this Celine Bergkamp will now prevent transport of the diversionary object from Germany. If Ms. Bergkamp should be unsuccessful, pertinent measures are planned along the transport route in Eastern Europe.

CHAPTER 43

Monday, late afternoon at Lake Wannsee. Having had enough for one day, I cleared out of Berlin South early.

I felt the frustrations of the day at the hospital falling away from me and being soaked up by the sandy beach. Directly across the lake, the sun was setting in an array of beautiful colors, painting the woods and the water in an almost supernatural light. Spring hadn't quite arrived yet, but a few sailboats were out, trying to reach port before the forecasted rain. At work that day, I'd had the pleasure of meeting our new department head. I still couldn't believe it! But that was irrelevant. The only important thing was that Celine was sitting beside me—and speaking to me.

I had skipped the morning conference at the hospital and instead busied myself with the towering stack of papers that awaited me on my desk, threatening to collapse any minute. It was the usual stuff: The insurance companies wanted to know why patient A or B with diagnosis X or Y had gotten treatment C rather than D and would I please care to explain. The Vitalis accounting department asked why the cost of treatment for patient E or F had been higher than what their insurance would reimburse us and would I please care to explain. My own insurance company reminded me that I still hadn't paid my malpractice insurance and that, according to paragraph XY-point-YZ, I was momentarily working without malpractice insurance. OK, the last item did have some urgency, and I took care of it. The rest could wait a little longer, as working through all of it would easily have taken all day and I would never have seen a single patient.

I heard a knock, and nurse Käthe stuck her head through the door.

"Dr. Hoffmann! Good to see you back! Our new department head wants me to ask you why you're not on rounds with him."

Käthe assumed that I had been informed who the new department head was. Which I hadn't been.

I had spent the whole weekend thinking about Celine, and had finally written and rewritten a long e-mail to her. I had blanked out the hospital completely, even when I heard Beate on my answering machine, asking me urgently to call her back.

I got up and followed Käthe. Suddenly, I knew exactly who I was about to meet. And I was correct! Rounds were already in full swing, and I just joined the procession.

"Herr Hoffmann! How nice of you to spend some of your precious time with us." This was how, two patient rooms later, I was greeted by Dr. Zentis, self-appointed specialist in terrorist plague-attacks, specialist in internal medicine with a questionable degree, and our new department head.

I continued to follow the procession without comment. After an absence of two weeks, I didn't have much to contribute anyway. I just listened to what the residents reported about the patients, and more particularly to what the patients told us themselves. I hardly knew any of them, since the average duration of a hospital stay in the internal medicine department was down to less than seven days. I also didn't know one of the doctors who was making rounds with us, and guessed that he was yet one more guest doctor from Arabia. Nobody bothered to introduce us.

After the parade, guest doctor Hassan had a few questions for me concerning the patients on dialysis. Unfortunately, Herr Krauskopf was still one of them. But I agreed that his laboratory results would allow us to put him on a less strict dialysis regimen. After we agreed on how to handle the other patients, I had the chance to ask him a question.

"So where's this new guest doctor from, Hassan?"

"From Iraq. He's a fellow countryman."

I found that astonishing. The pair hadn't uttered so much as a word to each other for the entire two hours that we had been strolling around the wards. But Hassan didn't elaborate further and instead asked me:

"Do you know our new department head from before?"

You could say that again! And also, that I had grossly underestimated him. Back in college, Zentis had been a decathlete of some repute in the lower leagues. Decathletes learn endurance. They also learn to pace themselves, they learn tactics, and, most important, they learn that the race is only over after the last event!

These were the qualities that had finally landed him the job of department head in the very hospital that only a few years earlier had fired him for incompetence! I would have seen it coming, or at least pricked up my ears, if he'd staged a little scientific symposium on some current medical question, which is the usual procedure if you want to make sure you're not overlooked during a department head search. But his variant—the exercise on bioterrorism—wasn't just new, it was ingenious. It not only got him the attention of the medical "in" crowd, but also those of politicians and the media. My questions at his press conference, or rather the questions "my" journalist had posed, evidently hadn't hurt him. Which was understandable, since the background information was simply too complex for the mainstream press.

Dr. Hassan was still looking me. Oh yes, his question.

"Yes, I know Herr Zentis. He used to work here as a doctor. I think he's a good choice for the job. I'm sure his excellent contacts in the departments of health and internal affairs will be a great help to the hospital."

"And on the medical side?"

While Zentis had been doing his first rounds as department head, Dr. Hassan and his colleagues had looked at me intermittently, waiting for me to step in when Zentis's limited medical competence became obvious.

"You know, Herr Hassan, not only the patient has to be kept alive in a hospital. The hospital itself has to survive, too. And that requires good politics and a good administrator. That's why Zentis is the right man for the job."

It had been a painful way for me to come to that conclusion, but it was true. In all my immodesty, I saw myself as ten times the better physician than Zentis, which still didn't make me a leading expert. But as department head, Zentis really was the right man. Hoffmann, on the other hand, would have been miscast. Welcome to the age of bureaucrats and operatives!

That was enough about our new department head, but Hassan had a surprise in store for me.

"By the way, Herr Hoffmann, I might have good news for you. From Iraq."

"Really?" Hassan had my full attention.

"My brother-in-law has a friend in the Iraqi military. This friend told him about a German woman who was being held in custody at a military installation just south of the thirty-sixth parallel, close to the no-fly zone and close to the Kurdish territory. About three weeks ago, this military complex was bombed by American planes, and many of our soldiers died. During the bombing, this woman from Germany had a chance to escape, my brother-in-law was told. I think this is the story my uncle hinted at the other day. Just imagine, Herr Hoffmann—it may have been your friend who escaped! It all fits. She's probably safely with her Kurdish friends now, or maybe even in Turkey already."

I remembered that it had been on the news, this bombing of an Iraqi military complex just south of the thirty-sixth parallel. In any case, it seemed that Abdul Hassan couldn't have been happier had this news been about his girlfriend or his sister. Had I been wrong to suspect him of being best friends with his country's leader, or at least with the acting ambassador?

That's what it looked like, because it was Baran and his people, not the Iraqis, who had stolen Herr Sommer's machine. But the Iraqis should have been the ones most interested in obtaining it. Yet nobody from the embassy had accepted my invitation to the chocolate factory. The only reason I could come up with for that was that they hadn't been informed, that Dr. Hassan had not passed the message along to either his embassy, or directly to Saddam's agents in Germany. I thanked Hassan heartily, but remained cautious and didn't tell him that Celine was already back in Germany. A precaution that was probably unnecessary, because he had a warning for me.

"One more thing, Herr Hoffmann. For the time being, you shouldn't tell anyone other than those you already have about your girlfriend and her project."

It seemed obvious that Hassan was referring to our new guest colleague from Iraq. Was he the missing link to the embassy? Or was I seeing ghosts? Was there no missing link at all? I thanked Hassan once more and withdrew to my office, where I continued to work through the bureaucratic backlog and to get worked up over our new department head. And then I got angry at myself for getting worked up over it.

But the day still had something painful in store for me. At lunch, I was just lining up in the cafeteria when I heard giggling and whispering behind me. I turned around. Nursing students, of course!

"Oh, Herr Doctor. Will you take us to the movies some day?"
I took a second look. It wasn't even the same girls who'd witnessed me leaving that porn theater. My cinematic preferences had evidently become general knowledge at Berlin South!

By then the sun was a giant ball of fire just above the horizon, and Lake Wannsee a copper-red ocean. The pines were waving in the growing wind, the forerunner of the approaching rain.

"And so you just walked off that military installation?"

"Well, of course I was scared shitless. But mainly because of the bombs exploding everywhere, the walls coming down, the fire. The Iraqi soldiers didn't even notice me. They were busy dragging their comrades out from under the ruins and putting out the fires. It was total chaos, and I didn't see anybody giving orders or coordinating the action. Maybe the bombs had gotten the officers? Anyway, I doubt anyone would have recognized me anyway. I looked like anybody else with my singed hair and soot-blackened face. So, yes, I just walked away."

I could picture it as though it were a movie: Celine boldly making her way through the chaos. Oh, Celine!

"What were you thinking? That you're immortal? That Iraqi solders don't shoot women?"

"I'll tell you what I thought of: Nothing. Nothing except that this was a great chance to escape. OK, I probably also thought that the war had begun. But apparently some American or British fighter planes were just annoyed by the Iraqi radar."

In spite of my post hoc concerns, I was glad that Celine was finally talking about what had happened to her in Iraq. She had gone through a lot, but unlike what I'd feared, she hadn't been tortured or raped. But then, why would they have tortured her? She didn't have any secret information to give them. She had only seen what she had transported for dear Herr Sommer and where it was going and that had to be kept secret. So either they would have had to kill her or just lock her away until either the poison gas had been used or the gracious grass of forgetfulness had grown over the matter and a good occasion for a prisoner exchange came up.

I then understood that Celine's sadness, or melancholy—so out of character for her—after her return from Iraq stemmed not from having experienced or witnessed terrible events. It must have been mainly from frustration and disappointment. That Herr Sommer and his friends had so misused her, had debased the hardship she went through on her journey. And probably from growing doubts about whether these transports were truly necessary. At least when the Kurds were getting tons of money from the Americans to support their military plans. On top of all that was the realization that war was imminent—and that neither she nor anybody else had an idea how to free the world and the Iraqi people from their mad dictator.

We didn't talk about what might have happened to her friend Heiner, who was still missing without a trace. That was surely another reason for her sadness, but I felt it was too early to talk about that yet.

"I'm just wondering why they came up with that story about you having thrown a bomb. Why not just let you disappear, period? Nobody who knew you in the slightest believed that bomb story anyway."

Celine smiled at me.

"Really?"

That's when I learned that Celine certainly did have it in her.

"Well, it was no bomb. It was a hand grenade, I think. There were crates of them all over the military compound, where they'd also built their poison-gas factory. I was just so mad! It was all for nothing, all just for a big scam! I thought I was done for at that point anyway, so why not make a statement? So I threw this thing—but nothing happened!"

"Nobody was hurt?"

"It didn't go off at all!"

"You have to pull the pin."

"Nobody told me."

The wind gusts had increased considerably, and the sun had long disappeared. It was time to get going. Almost at a run, I grabbed Celine's arm.

"I don't want to sound ungrateful, but now that you guys traded that atomizer for me, the Iraqis will get it, right?"

Celine smiled.

"Don't worry. A lot can happen on a transport like that. And even if the machine gets that far, it won't function properly."

Now the heavens opened, and the rain came down in buckets. We were drenched to the skin in minutes. Celine raised both her arms to the sky, her face up toward the rain. With the wind and rain raging in the pine trees, we had to shout at each other.

"I'm happy to be back!"

"So am I—because otherwise you couldn't have rescued me!"

"Right. I saved your butt. That's going to cost you."

"OK, let's say one dinner at Luigi's—but you're paying for dessert."

Celine turned her head to the side, seemingly weighing my offer, and then laughed.

"No deal! You pay for dessert."

It was the first time since she'd come back that I'd seen Celine really laughing. It was then that I knew that she would be all right again someday. As would I. As would our relationship. That is, if we didn't catch death in that cold early-spring rain.

March 19, 2003
News Special

US President Bush declares start of Iraq war

At 10:15 p.m. EST, President George W. Bush announced that he had ordered an "attack of opportunity" against targets in Iraq, thus launching Operation Iraqi Freedom. The president declared that the U.S. enters into military action "reluctantly," but that "the people of the United States and our friends and allies will not live at the mercy of an outlaw regime that threatens the peace with weapons of mass murder."

District Attorney's Office
Stuttgart, Germany
Press Release

Investigations against Sommer Inc. dropped

The Stuttgart district attorney's office has dropped its preliminary investigation against Sommer Inc., supplier of products for the oil-and-gas industry. Sommer Inc. was being investigated on charges of possible violation of the German War Weapons Control Act (Kriegswaffenkontrollgesetz) and charges of circumvention of embargo regulations against the Republic of Iraq (U.N. Resolutions 661 and 1409).

Initial suspicion that Sommer Inc. had produced technical equipment and machinery for large-scale industrial production of poison gas and organized the illegal transport of said equipment and machinery to Iraq was not confirmed. Following up on an anonymous tip, customs officials at the Austrian-Hungarian border indeed confiscated a high-powered atomizer, which can be used for large-scale industrial production of poison gas. But neither the place of origin nor the final destination of said apparatus could be established with absolute certainty.

The Economic Times
German industry expects to do good business in postwar reconstruction in Iraq

Berlin, from our own correspondent:
In spite of the political differences between Germany and the U.S. government over the Iraq War, German industry sees an opportunity to be significantly involved in postwar reconstruction in Iraq. Mr. Sommer, spokesman for the Association of Small and Medium Enterprises, pointed to the good reputation of German technologies and industrial products in the Middle East. Mechanical and plant engineering; the energy, chemistry, oil and gas industries; and the medical and pharmaceutical sectors would particularly profit, Sommer said. German business has a long-standing relationship with Iraq, and those ties have never been completely severed, which will now pay off, he emphasized. Iraqi oil production will soon be operational again, so there should be enough capital to finance the necessary investments.

AUTHOR'S ANNOTATIONS AND ACKNOWLEDGMENTS

It is true that, for legal purposes, "the characters and events portrayed in this book are fictitious."

To the best of my knowledge (or rather that of the Internet), the United Democrats of Kurdistan (NDK), the Kurdistan Liberation Soldiers (KLS), and the Kurdistan Freedom Army (KFA) do not exist. These names are fictitious and were not easy to come up with, because (fictitious!) CIA agent Thorne is correct when he says, "They have at least one party for every valley, and every one of those groups feels called to fight for a Kurdish nation." That means most combinations of the terms *Kurdish*, *Kurdistan*, and *liberation* are already in circulation.

There was also never a chocolate factory in the East Berlin neighborhood of Treptow, on Kiefholzstrasse, at the corner of Elsenstrasse. I changed the address of the factory because I found it unfair to blame the factory and its personnel for the shortages of raw material they had to live and work with in East Germany.

On the other hand, the above-cited legal statement doesn't mean that the events described in the book could not have taken place: Operation Topoff was, in fact, carried out in Denver,

Colorado, from May 20 through May 23, 2000. The operation was based on the premise that terrorists had released aerosols containing *Yersinia pestis*—plague bacteria—at the city's performing arts center. For the details of this operation, I must thank two colleagues: a Dr. Hoffman (!), Richard E. Hoffman, who was chief medical officer and state epidemiologist for the Colorado Department of Public Health and Environment during Operation Topoff, and Jane E. Norton, who was executive director of the Colorado Department of Public Health and Environment at the time.

There might be people who will argue that the legal basis for telephone tapping in Germany is far different from what is described in the book, which is true. But the real situation around this time was analyzed by Otto Backes and Christoph Gusy from the department of law at the University of Bielefeld, in Germany, in 2003. These authors found that of 554 cases of wiretapping by the police or internal security, only one quarter of them were legal!

Monitoring of worldwide telephone, fax, and data traffic as described in the book is the mission of the Echelon program, run by the National Security Agency (NSA) in the US, with its own satellites and listening stations in the relevant regions of the world. In Germany, this used to be "Hortensie III" at Bad Aibling, which relocated in September 2004 to Griesheim and is officially operated by the US Army Intelligence and Security Command (INSCOM).

International diplomatic communications are monitored by the Department of Defense Joint Operations Centre Chicksands (DODJOCC) in England. The signal intelligence people who work there are not without humor. In the lobby of their place of work, usually referred to as Building 600, a copy of the International Telecommunication Convention is pasted up on the wall, including article 37 of the convention (also signed by the United States and England), in which the signatories "agree to take all possible measures, compatible with the system of telecommunication used, with a view to ensuring the secrecy of international correspondence."

One more remark for the historical purist: in chapter 39, Felix Hoffmann refers to the famous quote "peace in our time." The author is aware of the fact that the British prime minister Neville Chamberlain, in his speech concerning the Munich agreement on September 30, 1938, spoke of "peace *for* our time." But Felix Hoffmann is a medical doctor, not a historian, so he misquotes Neville Chamberlain like almost everybody else.

Today, in January 2013, we all know that the casus belli that President George W. Bush referred to in his televised address on March 20, 2003—that Iraq had "weapons of mass murder"—was wrong. As far as I know, it has not been definitively established whether the president knew that from the outset or was misinformed, as he suggested after the presidential election of 2008, saying, "[My] biggest regret of all the presidency has to have been the intelligence failure in Iraq." Soon after the start of the Iraq War in 2003, I found two interesting statements from his administration. The US deputy defense secretary at the time, Paul Wolfowitz, said that weapons of mass destruction had been declared the motivation to go to war "for bureaucratic reasons," because it was "the one reason everyone could agree on." I found it even more noteworthy that then defense secretary Donald Rumsfeld suggested that Iraq may have destroyed its weapons of mass destruction before the war began, which is why they couldn't be found. This, I find, would be something entirely new to history: that a leader faced with the extinction of his regime and his very person would destroy his last trump card for this fight!

Enough history. Now, it is not entirely true that *all* "the characters portrayed in this book are fictitious." There are two exceptions: my friend Torsten Römer, a former colleague of mine from the X-ray department, and his wonderful wife, Anja, do in fact run the most agreeable and highly recommended hotel "Zum grünen Strand der Spree" in the Spreewald, some forty miles south of Berlin. And Uwe Lorenzen and his family do indeed run a store in Leck, Northern Germany, that reminds one of the general stores of days gone by. It is unbelievable how many varieties of specialty-food items, wines, and teas from all over the world are available in that little space!

Unlike *The Russian Donation* and *He Who Dies Last*, I undertook the translation of *101 Nights* myself. This, I am sure, meant some extra editing effort for Christina Henry de Tessan from Girl Friday Productions. Thank you, Christina, for your patience, diligence, and great work! And many thanks again to Gabriella Page-Fort from AmazonCrossing and her team for their wonderful work, too.

Christoph Spielberg, January 2013. Berlin, Germany

ABOUT THE AUTHOR

 Cardiologist and Agatha Christie Prize–winning author Christoph Spielberg lives in Berlin, Germany, where his mystery novels have gained national notoriety. Spielberg was awarded the prestigious Friedrich Glauser Prize from the German Crime Writers Association for *The Russian Donation*, the first in his Dr. Hoffmann crime series, which was warmly welcomed by US critics in English, including, among others, starred reviews in *Publishers Weekly* and *Booklist*, which called it a "cracking good thriller." Spielberg continues to draw on his medical experience for his novels and short stories and to provide medical care to his patients.